Benefactor to the Baroness

The Seductive Sleuths
Book 3

Melissa Kendall

Dragonblade Publishing, Inc. is an imprint of Kathryn Le Veque Novels, Inc.
P.O. Box 23
Moreno Valley, CA 92556
ceo@dragonbladepublishing.com

Produced in the United States of America

First Edition February 2025
Trade Paperback Edition

ARE YOU SIGNED UP FOR DRAGONBLADE'S BLOG?

You'll get the latest news and information on exclusive giveaways, exclusive excerpts, coming releases, sales, free books, cover reveals and more.

Check out our complete list of authors, too!

No spam, no junk. That's a promise!

Sign Up Here

www.dragonbladepublishing.com

Dearest Reader;

Thank you for your support of a small press. At Dragonblade Publishing, we strive to bring you the highest quality Historical Romance from some of the best authors in the business. Without your support, there is no 'us', so we sincerely hope you adore these stories and find some new favorite authors along the way.

Happy Reading!

CEO, Dragonblade Publishing

Additional Dragonblade books by Author Melissa Kendall

The Seductive Sleuths Series
Companion to the Count (Book 1)
Mentor to the Marquess (Book 2)
Benefactor to the Baroness (Book 3)

*This book is dedicated to all the girls
I had crushes on but never had the courage to approach.*

Chapter One

London, 1866

FONTAINE SHEPHERD, THE Dowager Lady Kerry, stood with her back straight and her hands clasped at her waist as Mr. Hill, the chair of the London Foundation for the Betterment of Destitute Orphans, hunched over his desk and flipped through the pages of her report with knobby, slightly trembling fingers. He adjusted the steel-framed spectacles perched precariously on his nose, then gave a rheumy cough, splattering his desk—and her report—with bits of saliva.

She tugged at the bodice of her dark-blue walking suit, feeling as if the tall bookcases that lined the walls on either side of her were inching closer with every passing second. Mr. Hill had opposed her appointment to the board of the foundation two years prior, although she didn't know if it was her parentage or her sex that offended him. She had only secured enough votes by befriending the treasurer, Mrs. Eris, a task which had required two weeks of carefully following the woman to afternoon teas, charity galas, and any other event that Mrs. Eris fancied.

Mr. Hill reached the end of her report, flipped the sheaf of papers over, and slid it back across his desk toward her. "Good."

She swallowed her initial response to that monosyllabic re-view of her painstaking work and inclined her head slightly. Mr. Hill was less than a year away from mandatory retirement. If everything went according to plan, he would endorse her candidacy as his successor, and then she would be in a position to bring about actual change. As chair, she would put an end to the foundation's long-held mandate that any recipient of their charity must show sufficient piety and freedom from vices. She knew better than anyone that the "undeserving poor" were the ones who required their help most of all.

Before her father had lifted her out of poverty, she had treated every meal as her last. She had never known when she might spend a night shivering with cold or hunger. Even decades later, she spent many restless nights feeling like she wasn't Lady Kerry, widow of the previous Baron Kerry, darling daughter of the Earl of Adeline, but only little Frannie, the matchstick girl.

"The orphanages are full," she said, proud when her voice did not waver in the slightest. Every movement, every word, of her speech had been practiced in front of her mirror weeks in advance of this meeting. "The streets of London are overwhelmed with orphans."

Her dream, one that she dared not voice in front of Mr. Hill, was to open a boarding school that would train and educate both wealthy and poor children. But she was a long way away from having enough funds to support such an endeavor.

Mr. Hill folded his fingers together. "I find no fault in your logic, Lady Kerry, especially since Mr. Blake's report mirrors yours."

Her pulse pounded at the back of her neck. Of course it did because Reginald Blake, Mr. Hill's cousin, a solicitor, and the only other member of the board who was under the age of sixty, cribbed from her at every opportunity. She would have raised his behavior to the board, but she had no doubt that under the current leadership, the board would invariably side with Mr. Blake. Not only because of his connection to Mr. Hill but also because so many of her peers looked down on her. As if by coming in contact with her, they were exposing themselves to the same noxious fumes that rose from the Thames and engulfed the poor area of the city.

She would show them she was more than a street child, but first, she had to convince Mr. Hill that she was the most appropriate choice to replace him, starting with earning his approval on her proposal.

"The Viscountess Briarwood did mention that she wanted the foundation to expand into more charitable ventures," Fontaine said, using the weapon she had reserved as a last resort. The Lord and Lady Briarwood were two of the foundation's most significant patrons. At their latest fundraiser, Fontaine had overheard Lady Briarwood tell Mr. Hill that she wanted them to spend more of the funds she provided on London's poor.

Mr. Hill pressed his lips together as a vein pulsed in his temple. "What do you suggest, precisely?"

If he had actually read her report, he would not have needed to ask, but she wouldn't let that small injustice bother her. "I propose that the foundation establish a branch in Canada. The new world hasn't been struck as badly by epidemics. We can transport children there and settle them in new situations."

She had visited the bustling city several times before her husband had died. Unlike the new Baron Kerry, her late husband's cousin, who preferred to spend his time drinking and gambling to excess, Malcom had loved the journey so much that she'd often wondered if he would have pursued life as a sailor were it not for his title. For that reason, and many others, she was certain he would have approved of sending children to Canada. The air was much fresher, and there were plenty of opportunities for older children to take on roles as maids or footmen in larger homes.

Assuming Mr. Hill approved her plan.

After a lengthy silence, in which Fontaine had to bite the inside of her cheek to stop from babbling reasons Halifax was the perfect place to send London's many unwanted orphans, Mr. Hill sighed, then flipped open her report and squinted at the first page. "Where do you propose we acquire these children?"

He was considering it!

She forced herself to stand as straight and tall as possible, even as her heart thundered in her chest, and rattled off several of London's more well-known orphanages, ones that were frequently supported by members of the peerage. As she spoke, the deep fissures on Mr. Hill's face eased. He did not need to know that she also intended to venture into workhouses in the East End. It was not as if he would have any part in managing the operation once it began. A man like Mr. Hill was content to make decisions, then step away, trusting others to execute his orders.

"You will do this by yourself?" Mr. Hill asked.

She heard the alarm in his voice and grasped for a suitable response. She hadn't anticipated that he would be so set upon seeing to her welfare—the poor, widowed, childless woman— that he would find a point of impropriety in her plan.

"O-Of course not," she said. "I will bring an escort."

"A companion?" Mr. Hill asked, leaning forward. "If you will not take my advice and remarry, then you should hire a companion." He opened a drawer in his desk and withdrew a bulging, leather purse. "In this situation, the foundation can provide the necessary support."

"That will not be required," she said, as he thumbed through a stack of bills thicker than her report. The infuriating man scrutinized every proposed increase in charitable expenses but seemed eager to supply her with funds for such a trivial matter.

"This woman will be involved in foundation business, Lady Kerry," Mr. Hill said.

The set of his shoulders told her this was not a battle she would win. The stuffy, old man couldn't resist meddling in her life. She inclined her head slightly. "Of course."

If it secured his support, she would obey his commands. Or, at least, pretend to. She had no desire to employ a gently bred woman to lounge around her home like a housecat. It would be much easier, and less disruptive, to *pretend* that she had hired such a woman. Mr. Hill, who rarely ventured beyond his home and the foundation's office, would never know the difference. If it became necessary to produce her "companion," she knew a dozen ladies who would play whatever role Fontaine asked of them without question, given sufficient monetary incentive.

Mr. Hill sniffed. "Far be it from me to get in the way of a woman who wishes to dedicate herself to the poor. You have my approval to access foundation funds to execute your plan. I will expect monthly reports."

Which you will not read, she thought as she glanced at the stack of papers she had painstakingly prepared sitting on his desk. Nevertheless, the buzzing in her chest intensified. She had succeeded and was one step closer to securing Mr. Hill's support.

"Of course. Thank you, sir."

She dipped into a deep curtsey, then turned and strolled out of Mr. Hill's office with her head held high.

Chapter Two

Six months later

WITH EVERY PASSING minute, Rosemary Summersby further regretted agreeing to attend the ladies' charity meeting. She shifted on the hard seat, trying to find a more comfortable position. The eye-watering smell of several strong perfumes wreathed around her, and the piercing cries of street vendors filtered in from outside.

Perhaps that was why every other lady who had arrived for the meeting was presently clustered on the other side of the room, leaving Rosemary to sit by herself in the center of the last row of chairs assembled in front of a podium. She would have joined them, if only to smile and nod, except that the ache in her right knee had started up again, and she steadfastly refused to allow anyone to see her stumble.

The only thing that kept her from rising and strolling out of the stuffy room was the promise she had made to her niece, the Viscountess Briarwood, that she would at least attempt to find some manner of activity to occupy her time. According to Saffron, it was not healthy for a woman of Rosemary's age to spend so much time by herself. Saffron's younger sister, Angelica, had even suggested that Rosemary consider remarrying. At three-and-forty, Angelica had said, Rosemary was not yet incapable of bearing children.

She was not entirely in opposition to this opinion. It was only that since her husband's death more than twenty years prior, she had yet to meet a man who elicited anything beyond a flicker of mild interest. Her attentions were invariably drawn in an entirely different direction, which meant that the few intimate relationships she'd formed over the past decade had required the utmost secrecy, even from her closest family.

She glanced toward a group of three ladies and sniffed. What manner of companionship could she possibly find in an association that allowed their members to wear *bloomers*? The soft, flowing garment granted greater freedom of movement, but it also accentuated the curves of a woman's legs and caused one to imagine what might lie beneath…but that was beside the point.

The door to the salon creaked open and a bearded man in a charcoal-gray suit sauntered in, drawing the attention of several ladies. He removed his black bowler hat and turned his head around, as if searching for someone. The slight upward tilt of his snub nose combined with the narrowing of his pale-blue eyes suggested he was as uncomfortable with the casual dress of the other occupants of the room as Rosemary.

He did not take a seat but immediately approached the timid Lady Mason, who had been loitering awkwardly by the refreshment table since Rosemary had arrived.

"There you are, my lady," the man exclaimed. "Lord Mason sent me to retrieve you."

The room fell to a hush. Lady Mason's fair complexion paled, and twin spots of red the same color as her gown appeared on her cheeks. She backed up until she bumped into the edge of the table, rattling several stacks of glasses. "Mr. Blake, you're our solicitor, not a manservant."

He stepped closer. "I'm your *husband*'s solicitor and legally, I have advised him he's within his rights to demand you come home." He reached for her and might have caught her, but for the intervention of a woman who rushed across the room and smacked the top of Mr. Blake's hands with a swish of her parasol.

"There will be none of that, sir," she said, positioning herself between Lady Mason and Mr. Blake.

A fluttering started in Rosemary's stomach and rose to her throat. There was no mistaking the brazen woman standing with her legs apart and a parasol held in both hands. It was the same lady Rosemary had been avoiding for months, because every time the Dowager Baroness Kerry looked her way, her tongue twisted in knots and all rational thought vanished from her mind. On this occasion, Lady Kerry wore navy bloomers that emphasized her narrow waist paired with a scarlet, woolen blouse trimmed in gold braid. The combination of controversial and fashionable continued in her silver-streaked black hair, simply parted at the center and smoothly pulled back into a chignon, topped with a distinctly masculine felt hat. She might have passed for a man in dim light if it weren't for her sparkling, diamond-and-gold earrings.

"Lady Kerry," Mr. Blake said, scorn dripping from his words. "I should not be surprised to find you are the leader of this..." He curled his lip. "*Ladies'* group."

Rosemary began to rise from her chair to come to Lady Kerry's aid before reminding herself that the conflict was none of her concern. She was not like her niece, who seemed to jump from one adventure to the next. Over the past several years, Saffron had unmasked the anonymous artist Ravenmore, fallen in love with the man behind the alias, and helped the then-Dowager Countess Allen stop a series of slanderous newspaper articles. But each success had been accompanied by moments of despair. It had broken Rosemary's heart to watch her niece tearfully resolve to become Lord Briarwood's mistress, and the future Lady Briarwood had been forced to endure weeks of being shamed by society before her reputation had been restored.

Rosemary much preferred her quiet life in her safe cottage, where she could not be similarly hurt, even if it meant she might never experience the kind of excitement her niece seemed to love.

"This is a private event, Mr. Blake," Lady Kerry said. She turned her parasol so the tip touched the ground. "As you are not a member, I must ask that you leave. You may speak to Lady Mason when our meeting concludes."

Mr. Blake's frown deepened. "I am tasked by my employer to retrieve his wayward wife. It would not be wise for you to interfere, *matchgirl*."

Lady Kerry stiffened as a shocked murmur rippled through the crowd. She had indeed been a match seller before her father, the Earl of Adeline, had lifted her out of poverty, claiming her as the child of his late mistress. Lady Fontaine Weston's subsequent introduction to society and marriage to the former Baron Kerry had been a ready source of gossip in the *ton*. Rosemary, newly widowed at the time of the scandal, recalled how the newspapers had transformed every minor *faux pas* by Lady Kerry into headline news. A raised voice over a gentleman at a dinner became a shouting match. A gown worn to the opera, only a few years out of fashion, became a threadbare embarrassment. Each incident further proof that Lady Kerry's inappropriate upbringing made her unsuited for polite society, no matter her father's title. One particular cartoon that had caused quite a stir had depicted Baron Kerry accepting a trunk full of matches from Lord Adeline as a dowry for his new wife.

Lady Kerry thumped her parasol on the ground like a cane. "Might I remind you, Mr. Blake, that this is a *ladies'* group?" She raised her eyebrows. "Unless you wish to become a member?"

Rosemary slapped a hand over her mouth but didn't quite stifle her snicker.

Mr. Blake's face turned deep magenta. Rather than respond, he swiped out a hand and caught Lady Kerry's parasol, then attempted to wrench it out of her grip. But instead of sending the woman staggering, or striking her with her own weapon, he ended up in a rather amusing game of tug of war.

Laughter erupted in the crowd, but cut off abruptly when Mr. Blake released his hold and lunged toward Lady Mason. She gave a shrill scream but was spared becoming the victim of Mr. Blake's attack by Lady Kerry, who launched herself in his path.

The resulting scuffle lasted only a few seconds, ending when Lady Kerry slammed her heel onto Mr. Blake's foot. He uttered a strangled curse before stumbling out the door.

The moment Mr. Blake was no longer present, the victorious Lady Kerry was mobbed by women chattering their questions and offering exclamations of admiration. The noise was nearly enough to give Rosemary a megrim. She pushed to her feet and said, in her most commanding voice, "Ladies!"

A dozen heads turned toward her, including that of Lady Kerry. The woman was even more striking in her rumpled state, with small tendrils of black hair floating around her flushed cheeks. Rosemary licked her lips. The words that usually came so naturally to her during moments of chaos flitted out of her mind in fits and starts like a leaf caught by a breeze.

"I-Is this not a meeting?" Rosemary asked. She grasped for the back of her chair to steady herself. "I do not believe we should allow a man to disrupt our schedule."

"She's right," Lady Kerry said. She tucked the ragged edge of her right sleeve away and strode confidently toward the podium. When she reached it, she straightened. "We have a matter of great importance to discuss today. If everyone would please be seated, we can begin."

The command in her tone had Rosemary falling back into her chair, and soon every seat was filled.

"As the designated speaker for this month's meeting," Lady Kerry said, "I wish to inform all of you about the dire situation in London's orphanages."

Several ladies around Rosemary groaned, and then a voice called out, "Again? That's all you ever want to talk about."

"The speaker gets to choose the topic," another voice said. "None of us wanted to hear your lecture on the etiquette of calling cards last week, Mrs. Gilly."

There was a smattering of laughter, then the room fell silent.

"Thank you, Lady Cowper," Lady Kerry said. "I'd like to report on the relocation scheme the Foundation for the Betterment of Destitute Orphans started earlier this year…"

She continued for some time, expanding upon reports from Halifax regarding the treatment of children. Rosemary paid little attention, enraptured as she was by the speaker. She had never met another woman with such natural leadership qualities. Had Lady Kerry been a man, she would have made a spectacular politician or military leader. But the circumstances of her birth combined with her sex meant she would never achieve that level of success.

Rosemary shook the foolish thoughts from her head. She had obviously been spending too much time with Lady Briarwood, who had become far more radical in her political views since she had given birth to a daughter. The viscountess had even convinced her husband to bring several proposals supporting the rights of women before Parliament, although all had been struck down. Her determination was admirable, if misplaced.

Lady Kerry finished her speech, no doubt having gained the support of a few of the ladies present. She stepped away from the podium, which seemed to be the sign that the meeting was adjourned, as the group quickly dispersed.

Rosemary rose to her feet. At least she could confirm to her niece that she had attended the event and had no desire to repeat the experience. She was simply not interested in championing a cause, unlike many other widows. They might fill their days with charities and fundraising, but Rosemary preferred to focus on matters much closer to home. For example, ensuring her grandniece, Daisy, was given a proper education.

Perhaps that was why Saffron had insisted she attend this event. She had been spending a fair amount of time with Daisy. Was Saffron too polite to tell her she was making a nuisance of herself?

She exited the salon onto the bustling, dusty street and resolved to purchase more books and painting supplies. If her niece did not want her around, then she would spend more time in her cottage. There were many ways to occupy one's time. She only needed to find them.

As a cab rattled up to stop in front of her, she caught a flash out of the corner of her eye. She turned her head slightly, then hissed in a breath. Mr. Blake stood in the shadowy alley beside the salon with hands in his pockets. He could've been waiting for a cab, or hiding from the ladies exiting the building, but some small part of her knew he was waiting for Lady Kerry.

She should have turned around and left. The way Lady Kerry had confronted Mr. Blake was proof enough of her competency. But as Mr. Blake peered around the edge of the salon, the driver of the cab slid down from his post, spat a chunk of tobacco, then said, "That Mr. Blake's a right bastard. Whatever he's up to, I wouldn't go interferin', if I were you."

It shouldn't have bothered her that the driver had surmised her inner conflict and had come to a similar conclusion. But nothing had ever bothered her more than when someone told her what not to do.

She heaved a frustrated sigh before waving the man and the cab away. She would make exactly one attempt to warn Lady Kerry, if the woman was even still inside the salon. If she had already departed or was not interested in hearing what Rosemary had to say, she could at least claim she had tried. That would salve her conscience.

But as she maneuvered across the street, the door to the salon opened and Lady Kerry stepped out wearing a dark-blue cloak about her shoulders, despite the unseasonably warm temperature. As Lady Kerry lifted the hood of her cloak over her head, Rosemary was struck anew by the lady's beauty. According to the standards of the *ton*, she was merely pretty, but Rosemary's own preferences had always been more in line with those of the ancient Egyptians, a shapely silhouette, strong features, and a full bosom. The few women who had shared her bed since her husband's death had met all the same criteria.

She realized she had stopped in the middle of the road and continued her determined march toward Lady Kerry. Unfortunately, her momentary lapse in focus had given Lady Kerry enough of a lead that Rosemary wasn't able to stop her before she walked past the spot where Mr. Blake was waiting.

"Lady Kerry!" she shouted, but it was too late. Mr. Blake lunged from the shadows, wrapped his arms around the woman, and dragged her back into the alley. Rosemary's stomach dropped, and she burst into a run. There were many awful things a man could do to a woman, especially one he felt had wronged him. One's title and status ceased being an effective deterrent when a man was provided with sufficient privacy, especially when there was no risk of an angry husband pursuing him later.

She reached the alley, only to find Lady Kerry standing over the crumpled body of Mr. Blake. Her hat was by her feet, the chignon at the back of her head was half-undone, and there was a silver hatpin clutched in her hand.

The tension that had wrapped around Rosemary drained away. Her initial assumption had been correct. Lady Kerry had not required her assistance. As the woman had not yet noticed her, she could back away and—*CLANG.*

She kicked a discarded can. Lady Kerry spun around and raised her fists to her chin like a boxer facing down an opponent. Although Rosemary couldn't imagine a boxer brandishing a hatpin as a weapon. When Lady Kerry's piercing gaze met Rosemary's, however, she dropped her posture and frowned. "Mrs. Summersby. What are you doing here?"

A dozen excuses popped into existence in her mind. Excuses that would not reveal that she had been watching the woman with more than a passing interest. But as she opened her mouth to coolly say that she had simply been passing by and would now leave Lady Kerry to her own, the truth came pouring out instead.

"I saw him waiting for you. I tried to follow, but you were too fast."

"Ah," Lady Kerry said. "Well, as you're here, would you

mind helping me fix the mess I've made of my hair?" She lifted her arm to the level of her shoulder and grazed her curls with her fingers. "This is as far as I can reach."

Rosemary stepped closer without realizing she was doing it. Lady Kerry had that impact on people, a kind of charisma that was impossible to resist. As her fingers touched the woman's curls, a shiver went up her arm. Lady Kerry's hair was incredibly soft and shiny, and such a beautiful shade of black. Rosemary had always wished she could achieve the same luster in her brown locks, but she had never been willing to try the different chemicals and formulations other ladies used to achieve that look. Without asking, she knew that Lady Kerry used no such techniques. Aside from the fact that her eyebrows were the same shade, she couldn't imagine the woman, who seemed so dedicated to helping others, covering her hair in paste in order to become more fashionable.

Rosemary accepted the hatpin from Lady Kerry and tucked it back into place. This was something with which she was well familiar, having assisted her nieces with their coiffure for years after they'd come to live with her upon the death of their parents at the tender ages of five and three-and-ten.

The man on the ground groaned, making Rosemary startle and nearly stab Lady Kerry. She hurriedly pushed everything into place, hooked her arm with Lady Kerry's, then hustled them out of the alley. Lady Kerry chuckled but did not resist.

When they had passed several streets together, Rosemary found she was annoyed. She had attempted a rescue and instead had become involved in some manner of sordid activity.

"Where shall we go?" Lady Kerry asked, amusement clear in her tone.

Rosemary huffed. "Anywhere that is far from here."

Lady Kerry's tinkling laugh sent another round of shivers up Rosemary's spine. The woman had no shame dressing in such scandalous garb. Acting as if she were the only person who cared about the welfare of orphans. Of course, she had the history of being an orphan herself, so it was no surprise that it was something she cared about, but—Rosemary clamped down on her thoughts. If she were speaking, she would've been rambling.

"You shouldn't have aggravated him," she said.

Lady Kerry sighed. "I understand you believe that, but I could not let him take Lady Mason. Her husband has done enough violence against her to last a lifetime. Several ladies, myself included, have been harboring her to keep them apart."

A ball formed in Rosemary's throat. She had assumed Lady Kerry had had her own interests at heart, showing herself as the leader of the group by kicking out Mr. Blake. She had not considered that it had not been for her own benefit, but entirely for Lady Mason's.

"I apologize," she said. "I should not have… assumed. It is rather a bad habit for me."

Saffron had often vexingly told her to stop pressing her own assumptions and beliefs upon others. But she had been raised in an era when obedience to one's elders was of the utmost importance, and maintaining a respectful social standing was paramount. Unlearning those behaviors and realizing how she had hurt both Saffron and Angelica had caused her no end of stress.

Lady Kerry chuckled. "I am used to it, Mrs. Summersby. But if you were scandalized by what happened at the salon or in the alley, I would recommend that you do not follow me to my next destination."

The same contrary nature that had caused Rosemary to come to Lady Kerry's aid determined her response.

"Where *are* you going?" she asked. Lady Kerry had taken charge of their direction and now Rosemary was more curious than concerned. The electrifying thrill that had filled her when she'd discovered Lady Kerry standing over Mr. Blake had not yet dissipated, and she found she didn't want it to.

Perhaps her niece was the one who had figured out something important. Saffron's constant adventure-seeking had always seemed inappropriate and ridiculous. Rosemary had never felt a desire to experience that same adventure… until she had seen Lady Kerry playing the dashing heroine, besting Mr. Blake without assistance.

Saffron had asked her to form relationships. To find something with which to occupy her time. Perhaps that is exactly what she would do.

"Whitechapel," Lady Kerry said, as if casually telling Rosemary what she had eaten that morning. As if being seen near a workhouse wouldn't be a scandal in and of itself.

"You cannot be serious," Rosemary said. "That is no place for a lady of your status." She could only imagine what the newspapers would write if they learned. Phrases like *matchstick girl returning home* and *Baroness Whitechapel* came easily to mind. She had no idea why she didn't bid Lady Kerry a good evening and walk away. The dowager baroness was clearly determined to see herself injured, parading about London in a scandalous outfit. Confronting men in salons. It had nothing to do with her, and yet Rosemary did not want to leave. She had not felt so invigorated in weeks.

"In any case, you do not need to follow me," Lady Kerry said.

A casual comment, but it sealed Rosemary's decision.

"The two of us will make less of a target than one alone," she said. "I cannot, in good conscience, allow you to traipse off into a dangerous area of the city by yourself."

Lady Kerry chuckled. "You are certainly determined. As you wish. Perhaps, however, we might take a cab, rather than walk the entire distance?"

That was something even Rosemary could agree to.

Chapter Three

FONTAINE WATCHED THE woman sitting across from her in the cramped cab with interest. Mrs. Summersby's cheeks were flushed, her lush lips were slightly parted, and there was a smear of soot just above her right elbow, marring her otherwise perfect complexion. She clutched her black-gloved hands in her lap and stared wide-eyed out the window, as if they were descending into hell and not simply the very fringes of Whitechapel.

Unfortunately, it was too late to turn around and deposit her in a more fashionable district, because Fontaine had an appointment to keep. At the previous month's meeting, Mrs. Eris had casually remarked that the latest batch of children they had sent to Halifax had been half the size of the previous. As Mr. Hill had not yet announced which candidate he officially supported as his replacement, enterprising and community-minded Fontaine had volunteered to source more orphans. When she inevitably took over as chair in four short weeks, she would steer the foundation toward supporting the poorest of London's inhabitants. Until then, she would doggedly pursue any venture that would encourage the other members of the board to vote in her favor.

She exhaled harshly out of her nose. The members of the *ton* could not see it, but in most cases, the only difference between the wealthy and the poor was the circumstances of their birth. It was that understanding that led her to spend most of her widow's portion on charity. The only items of true value she possessed were gifts from her late husband—a set of gold-and-diamond earrings, a matching necklace—as well as a ring her father had given her mother. The necklace she kept in a velvet-lined box in her bedroom, but the other items she wore daily.

"What business do you have in Whitechapel?" Mrs. Summersby asked.

Fontaine returned her attention to the woman, who was fashionable even in her plain, woolen gown. The cut of her bodice was of the latest style, her hair was decorated with delicately carved pearls, and she spoke as if she were being observed by society at all times.

Before today, Fontaine had never thought much of Mrs. Summersby beyond the occasional wince of sympathy when someone had commented upon her late nephew's carousing or, later, the family's dire financial situation. Fontaine had certainly never considered the outwardly stern Mrs. Summersby the kind of woman who would have chased her into an alley. But now that she knew Mrs. Summersby had hidden depths, she found herself curious to see what else the woman was hiding.

"It would be best if you remained in the carriage," Fontaine said. "The conditions in the workhouse are likely to shock you."

Mrs. Summersby narrowed her eyes. "I will be the judge of that."

Fontaine leaned back, more amused than annoyed. "As you wish."

The carriage rattled to a stop, and she opened the door to a familiar sight. A towering, brick building rose out of the earth, surrounded by wide swaths of gravel-filled land on all sides. It was a place she would never forget, as even decades after leaving its walls for good, she still had nightmares of being dragged along the path, kicking and screaming. During her younger years, she had usually been taken to an orphanage after being found on the street, but as she'd grown, it had more often been a workhouse instead, owing to appearing older than she'd been.

It was this very workhouse where she'd first been assigned

the job of matchstick seller. Any income she'd received had been taken and the few times she'd tried to hide some coins in her clothing instead of surrendering them, she'd invariably been discovered and beaten severely.

She'd survived, but so many other children still suffered. That was why she returned, week after week. As long as she had the means with which to rescue other children from this hell, she would do so.

She exited the carriage and attempted to close the door, but Mrs. Summersby elbowed her way out. A slight shudder was soon disguised by a stiffening of her shoulders and a jutting of her chin forward. Both signs that Mrs. Summersby would not be deterred.

With a resigned sigh, Fontaine looped their arms together and turned toward the workhouse. The building loomed over them as they approached, and the wind made a high-pitched sound as it flowed along the bricks, almost like a scream.

Fontaine gulped but forced her feet to keep moving. When they reached the steps, the old, oak door creaked open and the owner, Mr. Newton, stepped outside, wearing a well-tailored black suit. He was a head shorter than both Fontaine and Mrs. Summersby and stood with his arms stiff at his sides. As they climbed the steps to greet him, his lips thinned.

"Lady Kerry," Mr. Newton said. "Have you come to select more servants?"

His words dripped with skepticism. Mrs. Summersby huffed. Fontaine elbowed her in the ribs and raised her voice. "I am to acquire two today."

She had established the lie that she was staffing a summer house the foundation operated months ago, and so far, Mr. Newton had not questioned it. Based on previous interactions, two orphans were the most she would be able to negotiate using the funds she had on her person. Mr. Newton was a shrewd businessman, and his rates increased with each visit. Unfortunately, there was little she could do but bear the cost. Bartering might cause him to investigate her story, and Mr. Hill would be apoplectic if he learned how she was truly using the funds the foundation provided for her alleged "companion."

She could have found another workhouse in a different area of the city, one that would gladly offload children to her without payment, but the orphans in those workhouses were treated comparatively well, owing to the city workers who performed frequent inspections. Those children would survive without her intervention. They did not need her as the children of Whitechapel did.

"I have brought a friend with me," Fontaine said. "Mrs. Summersby, this is Mr. Newton."

The man gave a slight incline of his head.

Mrs. Summersby sniffed.

"Come this way," Mr. Newton said. "I will show you our latest stock."

Mrs. Summersby made a strangled sound of outrage. Fontaine squeezed her arm and pulled her forward. Objecting to Mr. Newton's crude description of the children would only show the man how desperate they were, which would likely cause him to increase his rates yet again. It might not have bothered her to pay him, except that she knew the funds would never benefit the poor children who lived within the building.

She distinctly remembered sleeping in the attic on mildewy cots piled on the ground, huddled together with the other orphans like puppies to keep warm in the winter and splayed as far apart as they could in the summer, sweating profusely. It was a wonder so many had survived.

"Prepare yourself," Fontaine whispered to Rosemary as they strode deeper into the house. The walls were stained with mold, the floor creaked with each step, and a putrid smell wreathed around them, forcing Fontaine to breathe shallowly through her mouth.

"Here they are," Mr. Newton said as they reached a door. He pushed it open, and Mrs. Summersby gasped.

There were four children. Two whom Fontaine guessed were over four-and-ten, and two who were eight or nine.

The children lay on thin mattresses in narrow beds and stared at her with sightless eyes. Their heads were shaved—a workhouse precaution against lice—and they were clothed in tattered, oversized rags.

"I will leave you to make your choice," Mr. Newton said.

When he closed the door, an older girl with sharp cheekbones and wide shoulders slid off her bed and approached them.

"Who are you?" she asked. She must have been new to the workhouse, as there was little fear in her voice or posture.

"I'm Fontaine, and this is Mrs. Summersby," Fontaine said.

"I'm Annie," the girl said. Then she pointed at the other children. "That's Peter, Winter, and Xavier."

Those were not their real names, of course. Fontaine didn't expect they would tell her their real names, even if she took them away. She was an unknown element. They might not even *know* their real names. She had been called "Frannie" until her father had found her and informed her that her birth name had been Fontaine.

The other children did not speak. They were almost unnaturally still, as if tensed to run at a moment's notice. Between their shaved heads and identical clothing, she could hardly tell them apart, but she made an effort.

Xavier was similar in age to Annie. He was short and stocky and had wrapped his arms around a pillow. Winter was likely a year or two younger and was lean and long-limbed, suggesting he might be preparing for a growth spurt. He picked at the paint on the frame of his bed and let the flakes fall to the floor. The youngest, Peter, glared at her with the expression of a boy who had seen much in his short life. The fuzzy hair on his head was slightly longer, but his eyebrows had been shaved off.

A thump came from upstairs, making Annie flinch. She scrambled back onto a mattress and watched Fontaine with wide, shining eyes.

"This is horrific," Mrs. Summersby said in a tight voice.

"These are the ones who are too young or weak to become matchstick girls or pickpockets," Fontaine found herself saying. "The older boys are sent to the army or to anyone seeking an apprentice. The older girls are prepared to enter service as maids of all work or nannies."

Sickness often tore through workhouses and left behind a huge number of dead. Mr. Newton would not spare a single shilling for medicine. The children who survived the fever and the conditions in the house were the strongest and would earn the most income.

"My father found me here," Fontaine said. "I was as weak as they are. He had been searching for me for months. His mistress had told him there was a child, but she had died and left me on the street before telling him where to find me." She smiled, remembering how imposing the Earl of Adeline had seemed when he had arrived at the Whitechapel workhouse. The other orphans had been afraid of him, but she'd met his gaze stubbornly, hiding the youngest children behind her, a mother hen even at her tender age. Only later had she learned he had seen immediately that she was his—they shared the same prominent nose, the same star-shaped birthmark on their necks. She supposed she should have been grateful that she had inherited little from her mother, a woman she barely remembered, or her father might not have recognized her.

As it was, the earl had taken her to his home that afternoon, where she'd been subjected to a bath, a meal, and an introduction to a governess—in that order. In the days that followed, she'd been forced to dress in fancy wear, sit for hours at a table, and listen to boring lectures on etiquette. She had tried to run away many times, but the earl, who felt duty to one's children was of the foremost importance, would not allow her to leave. Eventually, she relented, and even grew to love her father, although her stepmother and half-siblings despised her for her intrusion in their lives.

"How do you decide whom to take?" Mrs. Summersby asked.

Fontaine shrugged off the ghosts of her past and stepped closer to Mrs. Summersby so that they could speak without the children hearing. "I've been doing this long enough that I can tell which won't survive the long journey."

She wished she could rescue them all, but until she succeeded Mr. Hill, that was beyond her means. Of the four, Xavier and Peter had a blue tinge to their lips and breathed with shallow gasps. They were likely beyond her ability to help. That left Annie and Winter.

The door creaked open, and Mr. Newton entered. "Have you made your choices?"

She swallowed the lump in her throat and pointed to the children she recognized as the strongest. She wished she could reassure them, but they wouldn't believe anything she said. They had no reason to trust her.

Mr. Newton cleared his throat. "Would you rather not take these two boys? Their youth makes them quite desirable. They'll grow into strong workers."

She shouldn't have been surprised that he was trying to offload the sickest of the children.

"And spread illness throughout my household?" she said. "I think not."

It pained her to leave the boys behind, but she had to make the most use of her slim resources. Children died every day in Whitechapel. That was a cruel fact of life.

"Perhaps just the one boy, instead of the girl?" Mr. Newton asked. "My other customers find much more value in girls. I could give you a discount."

"Enough," Fontaine said sharply. Then she bit the inside of her cheek to keep from telling Mr. Newton exactly what she thought of his *other customers*.

"Lady Kerry has made up her mind," Mrs. Summersby said.

Mr. Newton narrowed his eyes and glanced around the room, as if searching for another excuse. Before he could come up with something, she turned and strode confidently down the hallway, forcing Mr. Newton to rush ahead of her.

"You know, you might not find as many next time," Mr. Newton said as they walked back down the stairs.

"What do you mean?" Fontaine asked. The way Mr. Newton had spoken suggested a sense of self-righteousness, as if he were smug that he had bested her. But there were always children on the street, always unwed mothers giving up their babies or leaving them on the steps of churches or orphanages. As cruel as it was, starvation was a powerful motivator.

"There are fewer orphans by the week," Mr. Newton said. He gave a scowl. "It is rather cutting into my profits."

"Where are they going?" Fontaine asked, although she didn't expect Mr. Newton would answer. He saw her as competition, despite her saying many times that she had no desire to profit off the backs of children. To Mr. Newton, her presence week after week in the workhouse could mean nothing else.

Mr. Newton shrugged. "I haven't the faintest idea. I do not go seeking supply. They are brought to me."

Such a cold reflection of the business of selling orphans, but if she expressed that sentiment, Mr. Newton would use her sympathy and anger to extort more money out of her. She had to maintain the illusion of a dispassionate woman who cared little for the children beyond what they could do for her. But what were the chances that the next time she returned, Peter and Xavier would be gone?

She couldn't leave them behind.

"You have convinced me, Mr. Newton," she said. "I will take the other two boys as well, if you believe the stock will be low on my next visit. I would not want my housekeeper to be vexed."

Mr. Newton's brows drew together. "If you wish, Lady Kerry." Then he named a sum, and the amount made her swallow heavily. It was three times her budget. She could barely sustain her lifestyle with the funds she had. It was not that she cared for the dresses and shoes and all other manner of things the *ton* insisted upon, but that she *required* these things. They were necessary for her to blend in. Without them, no one would believe she belonged. Then it would be even more difficult to convince the men and women of society to give up their money to support the foundation.

But she couldn't leave the children, either.

"Done," Fontaine said.

Mrs. Summersby gasped. "Lady Kerry, do not be so—"

"I will return tomorrow with the rest," Fontaine said as she laid a stack of bills into Mr. Newton's hand.

She wished she could take the children away at that very minute, but her carriage was barely large enough for two adults, and finding a cab in Whitechapel willing to transport four street children would be impossible. She would have to request one of the foundation's carriages. It would be difficult with such short notice, but she dared not wait any longer, as Mr. Newton's ominous warning made her suspect that if she did, the children might not be here for her to rescue.

Chapter Four

FONTAINE STARED AT the sour-faced Mrs. Eris, sitting in her usual place at the front desk of the headquarters of the Foundation for the Betterment of Destitute Orphans. The woman's curly, white hair was pinned tightly to her scalp and her thin lips were pursed in what seemed of late to be her permanent expression of disapproval.

"None at all?" Fontaine asked.

The older woman shook her head. "I'm terribly sorry, Lady Kerry, but Mr. Blake took the last carriage an hour ago." She gestured to a row of empty hooks on the wall behind her desk, which usually held the hats and coats of their drivers.

Fontaine clenched her back teeth. It had to have been Mr. Blake who had stymied her. Now she would have to reach out to her other contacts and hope someone would be sympathetic to her cause. But as she turned to leave, Mrs. Eris cleared her throat.

She reluctantly faced the foundation's treasurer. "Yes?"

The woman tapped her desk with her forefinger. "Have you received any communication from the Halifax branch this week?"

The careful way she'd phrased the question made Fontaine frown. "I have not."

Mrs. Eris crossed her arms. "That is… unfortunate."

It felt as if Mrs. Eris were dancing around a subject, and Fontaine had an unsettling suspicion what it might have been. "When did the last report arrive?"

Mrs. Eris pursed her lips and plucked at the cream lace adorning the front of her blouse. "Was it last week? No, that's not right." She pushed her chair back from her small desk and used her cane to rise to her feet. Fontaine knew better than to assist her. Mrs. Eris was fiercely independent, even in her late seventies. Fontaine had watched with glee in their last meeting as Mr. Blake had earned himself a cane thwack to the shin for asking Mrs. Eris if she wanted a blanket to guard her against the chill in the boardroom.

"I keep all the letters from the Halifax branch here," Mrs. Eris said as she toddled toward a varnished oak cabinet. She removed a key from her pocket and unlocked a drawer, then pulled it open and withdrew a thick stack of envelopes.

Fontaine shifted her weight from foot to foot as Mrs. Eris's hand trembled, but she waited until the very last moment to reach out as the stack slipped out of the older woman's grip.

"Oh, my," Mrs. Eris said. "Thank you, Lady Kerry. You have remarkable reflexes."

Fontaine gathered the fallen envelopes—now hopelessly out of order—shuffled them into a pile, and placed them in the center of Mrs. Eris's desk.

"Now, where were we?" Mrs. Eris removed a pair of spectacles from her pocket and perched them on the bridge of her thin nose. "Ah, yes, the correspondence. Let's see." She picked up the first envelope and drew it close to her face before putting it aside. "Not that one."

Fontaine tangled her hands in her skirts to keep from fidgeting. Mrs. Eris was one of the senior-most members of the foundation and therefore had significant influence over the board. Fontaine could not afford to let her impatience cause her to lose such a powerful ally.

"Here it is," Mrs. Eris said. She tucked her spectacles back into the breast pocket of her blouse and raised the envelope into the air. "Two weeks ago. I have received no letters since this one."

Two weeks. Mrs. Eris had kept critically important information about the state of the relocation scheme to herself for a fortnight. She resisted the urge to snatch the envelope and held out her hand, palm up. "May I see it?"

When Mrs. Eris obliged, Fontaine carefully pried open the cut end of the envelope and withdrew the folded sheet of vellum from inside with two fingers. Then she placed the letter on Mrs. Eris's desk and smoothed it out.

"That's all?" Fontaine asked as she reviewed the scant three lines of writing. In relatively terse words, the operator of the Halifax branch, Mr. Sellinger, assured Mrs. Eris as to the wellbeing of the latest batch of young boys and girls whom he had received and confirmed that there were more than enough applications locally to accept children into positions to justify the foundation sending more orphans.

Fontaine had visited Halifax herself a few times since the foundation had started the relocation scheme, crossing the ocean by steamships. Mr. Sellinger had always been quite moderate when it came to estimations, which made the letter she was reading even more unusual.

"What are these?" Fontaine asked, tapping a line of numbers and letters that took up the bottom half of the page.

"A summary of where the children have been placed," Mrs. Eris said. She pointed to the first column. "'F' is for farms, where they place most of the boys. 'H' is for households, where most of the girls work. There are several others, but those two make up the majority, as you can see."

"How many groups have we sent?" Fontaine asked. There was something about the numbers that bothered her.

"Four," Mrs. Eris responded promptly. "One hundred and seventy boys, and thirty-three girls." When Fontaine met Mrs. Eris's gaze, the woman huffed. "My body might be slow, but my mind is as sharp as yours."

Fontaine quickly dropped her gaze back to the desk and drew her index finger along the column of numbers, adding the sums in her head. When she reached the bottom, her suspicions were confirmed.

"There are twice that number listed in this table," Fontaine said.

Mrs. Eris grabbed the paper. "That cannot be right." She fumbled her spectacles back onto her nose and brought the letter close to her face. "Oh, my." She touched her fingers to her temple. "How did I miss it? Lady Kerry, I am terribly sorry. I-I must tell Mr. Hill at once."

It wasn't hard to imagine what he would say. The old man would insist that the entire scheme be investigated. He might even create a committee to inspect Fontaine's work. A committee that would undoubtedly include Mr. Blake, who would find any excuse to put her in Mr. Hill's bad books. She assumed he hadn't mentioned what had happened in the alley out of sheer embarrassment at being bested by a woman.

"Wait," Fontaine said, her mind buzzing with options. "I know Mr. Sellinger. There must be an explanation for the discrepancy. Mr. Hill is terribly busy with the upcoming election. We don't need to bother him with such a simple matter."

Mrs. Eris thumped her cane on the ground. "*Simple*, you say?"

"Certainly," Fontaine said. She gathered up the envelopes and returned them to the drawer where Mrs. Eris had stored them, then turned and held out her hand. "Lock these back away and let me sort out the problem. I am certain it is a minor matter. A miscommunication. It is nearly time for a visit to Halifax, anyway. I'll sort out whatever this is when I arrive."

It wasn't entirely untrue. She did have a first-class cabin booked on a ship leaving for Halifax. It just didn't depart for several weeks. She hadn't intended to go so long between trips, but she couldn't risk missing the board election at the end of the month.

Mrs. Eris removed her key from her pocket and stared at it, frowning. "I suppose…I could overlook this." She curled her fingers around the key. "I like this position, Lady Kerry. It keeps my mind active and gives me something to do. But my eyes are not as sharp as they once were. Perhaps it would be wise if I stepped down and let a younger member take over."

"A single mistake shouldn't be the end of a prosperous career. The writing was faint, the numbers hardly legible. What you need is a visit to an optician."

Mrs. Eris touched the pocket that held her spectacles. "I believe you are right. Although I'm not keen on letting you go about this yourself." She brightened. "Perhaps you could bring your companion."

"What compa—a clever idea that is," Fontaine said, barely catching herself from asking a question that would have landed her in a difficult situation with the board. She had almost forgotten that the funds Mr. Hill had been providing for the past six months were meant to be a salary for a companion. What would Mr. Hill—or Mrs. Eris—think if they learned she had spent that money while visiting workhouses? She would be kicked off the board, if not expelled from the foundation entirely.

A bead of sweat dripped down her back. "My companion, of course," Fontaine said. Then, to forestall any further questions, she added, "You can count on me. I will discover the source of the discrepancies."

Chapter Five

WHEN ROSEMARY FINALLY returned to her cottage, the sun was low in the sky, and she felt as if she had aged ten years. She had never been inside a workhouse before, nor had she ever considered what it might be like in such a place. She doubted she would ever forget the guarded expressions of the children in that cramped, dingy room.

It had pained her to leave Annie and the others there. A pain she never would have felt if Lady Kerry hadn't provoked her into action.

She removed her hat with a sigh. That was being unfair. She couldn't blame Lady Kerry for what had happened, even if she was daft for allowing Mr. Newton to fleece her. Several hundred pounds for children who didn't look as if they would survive a fortnight. Mr. Newton should have *paid* Lady Kerry to take the orphans. It would have saved him the paperwork and hassle of feeding and housing them.

Rosemary rubbed her throbbing temples and trudged into her lushly appointed drawing room. The silk curtains blew gently in the wind from the open window, which had a remarkable view of the grounds and the forest in the distance. In the morning, the sunlight spilled over the trees and painted the sky in a dozen hues. Saffron had asked her to move into the main house several times, but when she was in that house, she felt as if she were intruding. Saffron and her husband, Leo, deserved time to enjoy their lives without Rosemary, practically an old woman, hovering around them.

A gentle rap on the front door made Rosemary turn, but before she had taken two steps, her maid, Nelly, bustled out of the kitchen. The short woman wore a white-and-green-checkered apron over her plain, brown gown and had tucked a frilly, white cap over her mass of curly, brown hair.

"Were you expecting company, madam?" Nelly asked. She removed her apron, then hung it on a peg on the wall.

"Not today," Rosemary said. The only people who visited her in the cottage were her nieces and their families.

Nelly walked to the door, opened it, then dipped a curtsey. "Lady Briarwood."

Saffron entered, dressed in a lovely, sapphire, silk day dress. Her long, black hair was braided and piled atop her head, beneath a lace-edged felt hat.

"You returned late from the meeting, Aunt," Saffron said, clutching her white-gloved hands at her waist. "I was worried."

That was Saffron, always putting the needs of her family before her own. Knowing her niece, she had sat by the window and fretted for hours. Rosemary's stomach twisted. She had attended the event to appease her niece but had only made her worry.

"I was waylaid by the Dowager Lady Kerry after the meeting," Rosemary said. "We had a rather interesting afternoon."

"Oh?" Saffron leaned forward, her eyes wide. "What did you do?"

Saffron's tone was nonchalant, but Rosemary recognized the mischievous smile her niece wore. It was the same one she had used nearly fifteen years prior, at the dinner table, before Angelica had come sobbing to Rosemary, claiming that someone had stolen her favorite woolen blanket. The girls had been so jealous of each other in their youth. After that event, Rosemary had taken care to only purchase gifts for the girls in identical sets.

"Nothing of importance," Rosemary said. She had already

worried Saffron enough without revealing that she had visited a workhouse. Her niece likely wouldn't believe her if she admitted she had interrupted Lady Kerry mid-assault and then had agreed to follow the woman on a mission of charity.

Saffron made a soft sound of derision. "I don't know why I expected anything else. You would not recognize excitement if it leaped into your lap."

If Rosemary were a cat, the fur on her hackles would have risen. "As it happens, I spent my afternoon visiting a workhouse in Whitechapel."

Saffron's jaw dropped open before she snapped it shut. "You did *not* venture into Whitechapel."

Rosemary could barely believe she'd done it herself. She'd made it very clear to Saffron that she disapproved of her niece's continual involvement in matters that were none of her concern. Supporting charity was a respectable pursuit, but committing a significant amount of money to a single organization was foolish. One would achieve better results by investing one's time in matters of policy, or convincing other members of the peerage to support their causes. After all, how much could one person accomplish on their own?

She remembered how Lady Kerry had gathered the orphans to her. The dowager baroness had much in common with Saffron; they were both incapable of keeping themselves out of trouble.

"Lady Kerry must be a remarkable woman to have convinced you to join her," Saffron said with a sly smile.

Rosemary's cheeks burned, and she could not meet Saffron's gaze. She felt like a debutante being congratulated for securing her first suitor, as ridiculous as that was. Nothing untoward had happened between herself and Lady Kerry.

"Will you be attending the next meeting?" Saffron asked as she perched on the edge of a horsehair chair, one hand on her stomach. She had not yet fully recovered from the birth of her first child, which worried Rosemary further. It was difficult watching the girl she had raised struggle, especially when she knew further children were nearly guaranteed. She hoped Saffron's husband understood the trauma that many births had on a woman's body. The viscount seemed to truly love Saffron. She hoped that meant he would be circumspect.

"I believe I will," Rosemary said coolly. Then, to avoid hearing her niece speculate, she added, "The children I saw today, you couldn't even imagine the state they were in. I took one look at them and all I could see was…"

Young Saffron and Angelica huddled together in the center of the living room, staring at Rosemary with enormous eyes. Basil standing in front of them, his tiny fists balled, his lips screwed up as if trying desperately not to cry. The three of them, alone in the world, their parents and grandparents and uncle all dead. How could Rosemary say no when they had no one?

Especially when she had no one, either.

"You remembered taking us in," Saffron said. "Well, my intent was that you would find someone with whom to spend your time. I suppose that has been accomplished. I hope you won't be taking any more turns in Whitechapel, though."

Rosemary huffed. "Not only that, I intend to convince Lady Kerry of the foolishness of her plan. There are many ways to go about improving the lives of orphans in this city without risking one's own life."

She would convince the baroness to give up her reckless ventures into dangerous areas of the city and instead focus on making actual change. Between the two of them, they could fundraise enormous sums if they could convince the wealthiest of the *ton* to support a singular cause. There would be no more masquerading under cloaks, wearing scandalous bloomers.

They could achieve the same means by staying within the safety of their social equals or betters.

Chapter Six

FONTAINE ADJUSTED HER cloak and adopted a swaggering gait. With luck, her rough garb, the lack of a moon, and the fog that crept in from the banks of the Thames would combine to keep anyone from recognizing her as anything other than another sailor seeking a nightly diversion.

After her conversation with Mrs. Eris, she had convinced Lady Trello to allow her to use her carriage to transport the orphans in the morning, and then she'd spent the rest of the day slinking about London's rougher areas, searching for clues regarding the discrepancy of the Halifax report. She didn't want to consider that it was connected to what Mr. Newton had mentioned about there being fewer orphans than usual, but it seemed quite a large coincidence. For that reason, she couldn't trust the foundation employees with investigating, in case any of them were involved.

Someone had to know what was happening to London's orphans. They couldn't simply be disappearing. It was far more likely that they were being *taken*.

She just didn't know who was doing it.

Unfortunately, none of her sources had helped, except to confirm there weren't as many children moving through orphanages as in previous months or years. No one had an explanation, although the orphanages were relieved rather than concerned. Fewer children meant fewer mouths to feed with increasingly thin budgets.

As she trailed behind a crowd of drunken, piss-smelling men, she wondered what Mrs. Summersby would have said about her current activity. The woman had gone almost apoplectic when she'd learned that Fontaine was headed into Whitechapel. Any other gently bred woman would have immediately given her a cut direct, but not Mrs. Summersby. She had seemed almost defiant when Fontaine had suggested she not enter the workhouse.

The group of sailors she was tailing reached their destination, a squat building near the water. Fiddle music filtered out of the open door, loud enough to muffle the sound of the waves hitting the shore nearby, and the light blooming from the windows cast dancing shadows on the ground.

She wrapped her cloak more firmly around herself and pushed through the throng until she found an empty table, then she sat with her back to the corner. The building was packed with men shouting and drinking and playing cards. How they could hear anything over the cacophony of clinking glasses, stomping boots, and off-tune fiddle music was beyond her. She had to resist the urge to slap her palms over her ears. Yet when a barmaid approached her table, she spoke in such a way that it cut through the noise.

"What can I get'cha? Ale, food, or company?" She lifted one dark eyebrow, causing a fluttering to start in Fontaine's stomach. She might have been dressed like a man, but that didn't mean she could respond the way a man would. Rather than risk outing herself with her voice, she slid a few coins across the table and made a drinking motion.

"One ale for the silent stranger," the barmaid said, bending over to collect the coins, revealing ample cleavage.

Fontaine tried not to stare as the curvy barmaid sauntered back to the kitchen. It had been months since she'd last pleasured a woman—a seamstress with nimble fingers and an explosive temper—and the temptation to allow herself a night of freedom was strong. But even if the barmaid's preferences were compatible with her own, she hadn't come all the way to the docks to indulge herself. If she were caught, news would make it back to the foundation and she would be tossed out in a second. That wasn't even the worst-case scenario. Presented with an attractive woman, a drunk sailor might not let a title prevent him from acting on his baser urges.

Her skin pebbled as a muffled scream came from outside. The few women who dared to venture this close to the water understood the risks but were forced by circumstance or vice to ply their wares to sailors. Men who could take what they wanted, secure in the knowledge that they would leave port on their ships before suffering any consequences for their actions.

She shuddered, remembering a girl she had shared a room with for a fortnight during one of the rare times she hadn't been stuck in an orphanage or workhouse. The girl had called herself Charlene. Her pale-blonde curls and dark-blue eyes had made her popular on the street, until she'd ventured too close to the docks and had never been seen again.

Fontaine licked her dry lips and closed her eyes, listening to the various conversations going on around her. It took time, sorting through the different threads of speech at varying volumes, but she had done this often enough when she'd been a matchstick seller that she knew what to listen for. People who were up to no good didn't shout, didn't laugh loudly, didn't make themselves the center of attention. They slunk in the shadows and whispered. The quiet ones were the most dangerous, the ones she had to be careful to avoid.

She forced herself to take slow breaths of the sour-smelling air and tilted her head so that her hood covered her face. Eventually, she caught the tail end of a question that piqued her interest.

"The Whitechapel workhouse?"

She turned her head toward the direction of the speaker and found a group of four men sitting at a table. Their garments identified three of them as sailors, but the fourth was different. The last man, neither the shortest nor the burliest, had a wiry beard shot through liberally with silver, and he wore a wide-brimmed hat that obscured most of his face. As if sensing her attention, he turned and met her gaze.

A pulse of heat shot through her. She glanced down at her glass, staring at the small bubbles forming on the surface of her drink. There was a distinctive sound of a chair being shoved back, and the noise in the room seemed to dim. When she dared to look up, the man was walking toward her with the three sailors following. The crowd receded from them like the sea during low tide. Before she could scramble away, the man was standing in front of her, his hands on his hips.

"Was there something you wanted, lad?"

Fontaine froze. There was no other word for it. Her throat closed up and her skin went cold. Half the room was watching them with expressions ranging from mild interest to excitement, and the other half carefully turned away, as if expecting a fight.

The man grinned, revealing several gleaming, gold teeth. "I see. No lad, then."

He'd seen through her disguise. She slipped her hand beneath her cloak and fingered the hilt of a dagger tied to her belt. The odds were stacked against her, but she would not allow these men to take her without a fight.

The man leaned toward her. "You have one chance, madam. If I dislike what you have to say, my men will escort you back to wherever you belong."

One chance to get him to tell her whatever he knew about the Whitechapel workhouse. She could have made something up, claimed she was a member of the *ton* seeking a thrill by venturing into the rougher areas of the city. But then her risk would have earned her nothing. As her plan had already failed, she saw no reason not to lay all her cards on the table.

"Children are disappearing from the street," she said, having to shout to hear herself above the crowd. "I want to know why."

The man jerked his head toward the door. "Come with me."

She stiffened. How many men had whispered words like that to her as a young girl, only to take what they wanted the moment they were alone? She shook her head back and forth while curling her fingers more securely around the hilt of her dagger.

"Ah. I see." He cleared his throat. "I can only offer you my word that neither me nor any man under my command will lay a hand on you."

She slid her dagger out of its sheath. "How do I know I can trust you?"

"A captain never breaks his word." He removed his hat and bowed in a sweeping gesture. "Captain Charles, at your service."

The fine hairs on the back of her neck rose. The entire room was silent and even the bartender had vanished from his post.

The captain replaced his hat, then turned to the man nearest to him. "Give me your rifle."

She scrambled out of her seat, only to have Captain Charles shove an enormous weapon toward her, butt first. She stared at it for several long seconds before wrapping her fingers around the handle.

"Be careful with that," the captain said. "It's primed and ready."

She flicked the chamber open to confirm, then settled the weapon more securely in her hands. Its weight was reassuring.

"Will that assure you I have no ill intentions?" Captain Charles asked wryly.

She nodded, then found herself trailing behind the captain and his sailors without considering what she might be getting herself into. She knew nothing about this man. He could lead her to his ship, where his crew would truss her up and throw her in a cage. But it was too late to change her mind. She was outnumbered four to one.

As they exited the building, a gust of wind tore at her hat and made her shiver. One of the sailors, a bald man with an eyepatch over his left eye and a thick bundle of fabric wrapped about his neck, pressed closer to her.

"Beggin' your pardon, madam, but you're looking mighty chilled." He unwound his long scarf and thrust it toward her.

"T-Thank y-you," she said, teeth chattering from both the cold and nerves. She accepted the offering and let out a soft gasp at the softness of the fabric. This was no sloppily knit item purchased for a penny out of a bargain bin. As she slipped it around her shoulders, she caught the sailor who had given it to her blushing. Before she had time to react to that, the captain came to an abrupt halt. The sailors turned their backs, forming an impenetrable wall around them.

"Cake is soft on you," the captain said, his expression unreadable in the darkness.

Fontaine took a step back. "I beg your pardon?"

What did confectionery have to do with anything?

The captain jerked his chin toward the back of the bald sailor. "Cake."

The sailor was named Cake.

A giggle burst out of her lips before she could hold it back. "I apologize, sir. I appreciate the gift."

"Just 'captain,'" he said. "I haven't been 'sir' in years." He tucked his thumbs into his belt. "I don't ask for formality from anyone but my men. Now, what's this about you hunting down children?"

She licked her suddenly dry lips. "I may look like a gently bred woman to you, sir—Captain Charles, but I spent my life on the street. I know how many urchins should be running about, after last year's epidemic."

The captain shook his head. "You're right about that. It's a shame what's been happening."

She stepped closer, her pulse pounding in her ears. "What do you know about it?"

He shook his head. "Unfamiliar faces lurking about. Ships that have no right setting off when they do. Not something I wanted to get tangled up in, but curiosity is a mighty beast." He stuck his hand in his pocket and removed a scrap of paper, which he held out to her. "I sent my first mate to speak to the officials who oversee this dock, and he brought me back this."

She peered at the tiny script. The writing was messy and slanted, the words difficult to make out.

"It's a manifest," Captain Charles said. "Reporting two dozen child passengers departing this port last week."

With that context, she could make sense of what she was reading. The name of the ship that had transported the children was missing, but there was something else scrawled at the bottom. As she tilted the paper in the faint light, she recognized several words.

"The Halifax Home for Destitute Children," the captain said. "That's where they're sending them. Can't say I know what that place is, although we've been to Halifax often enough delivering goods."

She gulped. It was as she'd feared. Mrs. Eris had told her that the foundation had only arranged for four groups of children to be transported over the past several months, but it appeared that someone else was also supplying the Halifax branch. That explained why Mrs. Eris had miscalculated.

"Thank you," Fontaine said. "I…will investigate this further."

She tried to imbue her words with confidence, but internally, she quaked. She couldn't tell Mrs. Eris about what she'd found, or the woman would certainly involve Mr. Hill. Then the careful plans she had been forming over the past year would crumble like a sandcastle washed away by the sea. Mr. Hill would demand a review of the program, and any failings would surely reflect on her. The chance she had of usurping leadership of the board would vanish. She had to sort this mess out herself before Mr. Hill retired at the end of the month without raising the suspicions of anyone else at the foundation.

If only she could speak to Mr. Sellinger. She had already penned a letter requesting a status report, after speaking to Mrs. Eris, but it would take ten days for her letter to reach its destination, and just as long to receive a response. What she needed was a more direct method of communication. To learn for herself what had happened and untangle the mess of miscommunication before anyone thought to investigate. The only trouble was that her usual transport was not due to leave for weeks.

"You about done, cap'n?" Cake asked. "I promised Cookie a match before we set off for Halifax."

Could the answer to her problem be standing right in front of her?

"How long is your passage across the ocean?" she asked.

The captain narrowed his eyes. "It's just over a week to get there, in good weather. Then I grant the men a few days' leave before returning. Why do you ask?"

She did the calculations swiftly in her head. If she was lucky, she would have just enough time. She reached into her pockets for the stack of bills she'd intended to use as bribes. "Would you be amenable to taking on another passenger?"

He accepted the money she thrust toward him with a scowl. "A single woman traveling alone? That's a disaster in the making, madam." But he didn't immediately give the notes back.

A *single* woman. Just like Mrs. Eris, the captain did not approve of her acting on her own. It was almost enough to make her wish she had remarried, although she doubted a husband would have allowed her to lurk around the city in disguise. Even Malcom, who had delighted in hearing exciting stories from her youth, would have disapproved. Then a sudden, wild impulse possessed her, and she straightened.

"Fare for two passengers. I travel with my companion."

A companion who didn't exist. What was she thinking? She hardly had time to pack for a three-week voyage, much less hire a woman to accompany her. It was unfortunate that Jones had left to be married. Since the baron's death, her former lady's maid had accompanied Fontaine on all her voyages across the ocean until now. There was no room in her budget to hire a replacement for Jones, after purchasing the orphans. Where would she even find someone willing to jump on board a ship with little warning?

"I suppose…" The captain tucked the bills into his pocket. "Be ready Wednesday afternoon. We'll be leaving with or without you."

Chapter Seven

ROSEMARY JERKED UPRIGHT in bed. Her face was covered in a sheen of sweat and the room was uncomfortably warm. A sound came from outside, a kind of moaning, and then a knocking, like a woodpecker, but at an odd interval. Her heart thudded in her chest as she curled beneath her blankets, the fog of sleep still obscuring her thoughts. She should do something. Rise and peer out the window? Or pretend to ignore the sound and go back to sleep, assuming it would stop?

But if there really was someone outside, what was stopping them from barging in? Even living with only one maid, she had never felt unsafe, as her cottage was fairly remote, on the far edge of the Briarwood estate. The only people who ever ventured near were the staff and the occasional villager.

The rapping came again, followed by a moan.

What if there was a highwayman, a brigand, or someone who wanted to steal from her?

She threw the thin blanket off her legs and crept to the window. When she peered outside, her heart leaped into her throat. A black-cloaked figure leaned against the outside of her cottage. Then the figure spun around and, in that moment, the terror that had filled her vanished, replaced by a searing heat that spread from her chest down her legs. The stranger was no bandit, but Dowager Baroness Kerry.

Lady Kerry was outside her cottage.

She rushed to open the door. It was raining, but not a heavy downpour. Just enough that as Lady Kerry stumbled inside, she left a puddle of muddy water in her wake. Beneath her robe, she wore an orange day dress with a full skirt, cap sleeves decorated with black, knitted lace, and a bonnet covered in orange ribbon tied in bows. As she removed her cloak, she wavered on her feet, and the smell that radiated from her was distinctly alcoholic.

Lady Kerry was drunk.

What was the proper decorum for managing a drunk woman of higher social status who appeared at one's door in the small hours? The situation was certainly one in which many other ladies would have squealed with delight to find themselves, as when Lady Kerry regained her senses, she would certainly owe Rosemary a significant apology and a boon, unless she wanted news of her escapades to ripple through the *ton*. Not that Rosemary would have considered indulging in such a thing. Only the cowardly used blackmail to accomplish their goals.

"I apologize for coming to see you at such a scandalous hour, Mrs. Summersby," Lady Kerry said, slurring her words only slightly. "I have something I must speak to you about."

Rosemary turned to the side so the woman could enter. The small space did not quite allow her to move far enough away, so when Lady Kerry walked past her, the hem of her orange skirt flirted over the edge of Rosemary's feet.

Her cheeks burned, and she chastised herself for her entirely unacceptable infatuation with the baroness. Nothing could come of such feelings. They were both women. Being caught engaging in intimate matters with another woman, especially a member of the peerage, would only result in them both being cast out of society. Rosemary had engaged in short-term intimate relationships with lower-class women in the past, but they had inevitably ended when it had become too difficult to keep the secret. She was too old and too tired for such things now.

She realized Fontaine was speaking and forced her attention back to the baroness.

"...no choice," Lady Kerry said as she paced the cottage. "If Mr. Hill finds out, he'll expel me from the board."

"Mr. Hill?" Rosemary asked as she returned to her chair. She didn't attempt to stop her unexpected visitor. Doing so would have been an exercise in futility. The woman was obviously overset and needed some time to vent her anger.

At least they had not yet woken Nelly. Rosemary would have struggled to explain to her maid why a dowager baroness was visiting the cottage in the middle of the night. The only thing that would've been more scandalous was if Lady Kerry were a man. Rosemary had struggled with her nieces allowing themselves to be placed in similar positions with men before they had married. It had taken all of her restraint to stop herself from locking the girls in their rooms.

That was irrelevant now, though. Both of her nieces were wed, and both were with child, or a mother already. There was nothing left for Rosemary to do. Her duty was complete.

Lady Kerry buried her fingers in her hair. "Insufferably proper arsehole. If I even step a toe out of line, he chastises me." She uttered a strangled scream. "I'm so sick of it. Sick of playing his game. One more month, and then he'll be out, but what of me? There's no time. I don't know what to do."

To Rosemary's horror, tears ran down Lady Kerry's cheeks.

"I apologize, but I haven't the faintest idea what you are talking about," Rosemary said. Then she softened her tone. "What happened?"

"So many children," Lady Kerry said on a sob. "I've failed them all."

The muscles in Rosemary's shoulders tensed. "Annie and the others?" She would never forget how the poor orphans had clung to each other in the cramped room. It would break her heart to learn that something had happened to them, even though she'd only met them hours ago.

That was the danger of getting oneself involved. It became much more difficult to maintain the necessary emotional distance. Now that she knew the names of the orphans, she couldn't forget them.

Lady Kerry brushed her cheeks with her gloved hands. "Not Annie and the others. I'll be picking them up tomorrow and taking them to one of the foundation's homes. But others have been taken from the street and transported to the new world. I've had no luck trying to track down what gang is doing it. That is why"—she met Rosemary's gaze—"I've decided I have to see for myself. I have a ship willing to transport me to Halifax, but the captain won't take me unless a lady comes with me."

Several seconds passed before Rosemary realized Fontaine was done speaking, then the implication of her words hit her like a punch to the throat. "You want *me* to accompany you across the ocean?" The request was so absurd, it was not even worth considering. She was content in her cottage. She did not need to experience the adventures her nieces had involved themselves in throughout the previous several years. Her life was interesting and satisfying enough, without excitement.

Maybe if she kept telling herself that, she would believe it.

Lady Kerry shook her head. "You are right, of course. I'm sorry. I should not have come here. It was unfair of me to involve you in such matters." She chuckled. "The eminently proper Mrs. Summersby, traveling to Halifax at the drop of a hat. What was I thinking?"

At those words, the contrary creature inside of Rosemary awoke from slumber and reared its head. Lady Kerry's scorn, her quick dismissal before even receiving a response, rubbed against Rosemary like coarse wool on freshly bathed skin. Why *shouldn't* she have her own adventure?

Saffron's words from that afternoon returned to her in a flash.

"You would not recognize excitement if it leaped into your lap."

What would Saffron and Angelica say if they learned their aunt had abandoned her new "friend" to her own affairs, despite knowing that Lady Kerry could likely get herself in significant trouble?

"Wait," Rosemary said before she realized what she was doing. Lady Kerry seemed to draw an impulsive urge out of her, which was both thrilling and terrifying. "Are you certain the children are coming to harm?"

Lady Kerry chewed on her lower lip. "The Halifax branch has stopped responding to letters and telegrams." She pressed her fists to her temple. "I established the relocation scheme, Mrs. Summersby. It was on my orders that the foundation sent children. If something has happened to them..." Her shoulders slumped. "I have witnessed the worst of what can befall street urchins. Fates I wouldn't wish upon my worst enemy."

Rosemary gulped. She had almost forgotten that Lady Kerry had not always been a lady and had likely suffered more than anyone Rosemary had ever met. Despite that, Lady Kerry didn't seem to grasp the danger of her plan. She might be scammed, or worse, once she arrived in Halifax.

Rosemary remembered what she'd told Saffron earlier, that she'd attempt to convince Lady Kerry to focus on more socially acceptable ways of achieving her goals. This was a perfect time to start.

"There must be someone else you can send," Rosemary said. "Why must you do this yourself?"

Lady Kerry threw up her arms. "Don't you understand? If I've allowed those children to come to harm..." She put her hands over her face. "I would never forgive myself."

Lady Kerry was somehow even more beautiful in her misery, with flashing eyes and flushed cheeks. Rosemary wanted nothing more than to pull the woman into an embrace and mutter nonsense words until Lady Kerry calmed down. But she dared not risk such a display of affection when any of her guests might see them. She wasn't quite ready for any of them to learn that secret.

Suddenly, she remembered how she had initially rejected Angelica, Saffron, and Basil. The children had not been her responsibility. She wasn't related to them by blood. She had sent the solicitor who had come to her door away, certain that someone else would take in the children. If she hadn't changed her mind, they could have ended up with their distant cousin, who had inherited the baronet title after Basil's death. The man might have done nothing for the children beyond the bare minimum required by the law.

She could not fault Lady Kerry for her dedication to children for whom she obviously felt responsible. Rosemary had been in such a place and had made the same decision. One that she had never expected to make but did not regret.

Still, a trip to *Halifax*? Canada?

It was ridiculous. There had to be another way, even if Lady Kerry could not see it.

"I will accompany you to retrieve the children from the Whitechapel workhouse," she said. "After we've secured them, then I will consider your…other request."

During their trip to the workhouse, she would use every argument she could think of to make Lady Kerry realize she had other options available to further her goals. There was no need for her to do everything on her own.

"You will not regret this," Lady Kerry said. Then she threw her arms around Rosemary's neck, causing her to imagine many impossible things, such as lying in bed with Lady Kerry curled up against her, their tangled limbs slick with sweat.

She mentally shook herself. Lady Kerry was a virtual stranger, a dowager baroness and the daughter of an earl, a woman who had shown no sign that she was interested in anything more from Rosemary than companionship.

Unless that changed, she would not allow herself to consider scenarios that could never happen.

Chapter Eight

FOR THE SECOND time in as many days, Fontaine sat in a carriage across from Mrs. Summersby, whose long-sleeved, muddy-brown, cambric gown clasped her in a drab embrace. This was in sharp contrast to the lacy nightgown that she had worn in Fontaine's dreams the previous night, where Mrs. Summersby had twisted her hips in a motion that even now had Fontaine squirming in her seat.

It wasn't right, imagining her apparent new friend in such licentious scenarios, but when Mrs. Summersby had held her, it had felt so *right*. Like she had finally found something she'd wanted since she'd been a young woman but had never dared to pursue.

The freedom to choose.

Her whole life among the social elite had been planned, starting from the moment her father had plucked her from obscurity. After she'd recovered from the shock and anger of learning her true identity, she'd realized how much she owed him and had resolved to obey the earl's every command. If he wanted her to attend a finishing school with dozens of other girls who cared nothing for her beyond her connections, she would attend. If he wanted her to become the darling of her first season, she would throw herself into learning the complicated social games required to fit in with the *ton*. If he wanted her to marry, she would walk joyfully down the wedding aisle.

It was not as if marriage had been terrible. She had enjoyed Malcom's companionship, even if he had rarely come to her bed. However, remembering her husband's affections did little to stir her passions, whereas the very thought of Mrs. Summersby sent her skin aflame. It was a pointless attraction—Mrs. Summersby was as stoic and as proper as any society lady and would likely gasp at the mere mention of anything sapphic—but one could not deny one's own desires.

"I believe we have arrived," Rosemary said.

Fontaine jerked her head toward the window. The carriage had indeed stopped. In moments, they were once again walking up the long path to the Whitechapel workhouse. The smog that emanated from the chimneys fouled the air, making Rosemary cough. Even Fontaine was affected, even though she'd once lived with dozens of other children ranging from infants to nearly adult, with few opportunities to bathe.

"Press your handkerchief to your nose if it becomes too much," Fontaine said as she noticed Mrs. Summersby's eyes watering.

It was hard to believe the woman had agreed to come with her on this second trip. Fontaine was well aware that most of the *ton* had looked down upon her from the moment she had entered their ranks. It was as if the day one was born, a seal was placed upon the potential of a person, and one could never strive to exceed that potential.

But Fontaine was very good at breaking into, and out of, all manner of things.

"How many children do you think have come through this place?" Mrs. Summersby asked.

"Thousands," Fontaine said, linking their arms.

"Will it..." Mrs. Summersby gulped. "Will it be as bad as last time?"

"It will be worse. Some of them might have even died. These places"—she jerked her head toward the towering, stone building—"are designed to break spirits. No one wants to be here, least of all children."

Mrs. Summersby stopped walking, forcing Fontaine to do the same.

"You could wait in the carriage," Fontaine said gently.

Mrs. Summersby closed her eyes, straightened her shoulders, then shook her head. "No. Let us do this while I still have the strength."

Fontaine's heart swelled. Even if Mrs. Summersby didn't agree to accompany her to Halifax, she hoped they would remain friends. It was rare to find anyone with such courage.

If Mrs. Summersby balked at the request, she wasn't sure who else she could ask. There were only so many ladies in London who wouldn't laugh at such a proposition. She might hire a new lady's maid, but there was so little time. When she tried to imagine a stranger standing beside her on the docks, the unknown woman invariably transformed back into Mrs. Summersby.

They climbed the steps to the workhouse, but before she could knock, the door flew open, and Mr. Newton stumbled out. His shirt gaped, and a wrinkled neck cloth was slung over his shoulder. She had never seen him in such a state before. He was always impeccably dressed for her visits.

"L-Lady Kerry," he said. "What are you doing here?"

She removed a stack of bills from her pocket. "I am here to collect the orphans."

He shook his head. "You cannot."

So, he was going to demand more money. With Mrs. Summersby standing firm at her side, she would summon the strength to stop Mr. Newton from extorting her further.

"The orphans," she said, holding out the bills.

"Get out of here, woman!" He smacked her hand. "Take your money and leave."

Mrs. Summersby gasped. "Mr. Newton!"

The bills fluttered to the ground. Rosemary knelt and snatched them up, getting dirt on her dress in the process. Then she offered them to Fontaine, who shoved them back in her pocket.

"Never come back here," Mr. Newton said. He took several steps backward into the workhouse, then slammed the door.

Fontaine's vision darkened for a moment. It felt as though someone had reached inside her chest and wrenched out her heart. The next thing she knew, Mrs. Summersby was dragging her back toward the carriage. Fontaine peered over her shoulder. A light flickered on in a window on the second floor of the workhouse and several faces peered out.

The children.

She'd come to deliver them to a better life, as her father had done for her.

"I can't leave them," Fontaine said, without taking her gaze off the window, which was growing smaller by the second.

Leave no one behind. That was the rule of the street.

Except she *had* left them behind.

When her father had rescued her, she'd turned her back on her people in an instant and hadn't returned to visit them until after Malcom's death. It wasn't that her husband had forbidden her from visiting Whitechapel, but that she'd wanted to forget she'd ever been "Frannie," outside of the occasional story he'd found fascinating when they'd been alone. Her new wealthy friends and elegant surroundings had made her feel guilty and ashamed, and it had been easier to bury those feelings than confront them. It had taken the losses of both her husband and father in short succession for her to realize that she'd become one of the willfully ignorant nobs whom Frannie had once ridiculed.

Mrs. Summersby ushered her into the carriage, blocking her view of the workhouse.

She clenched her hands in her skirts. "I told them I would take them. I promised them." She wanted to run back up the path, throw open the doors, find the children, and gather them into her arms. But her limbs felt impossibly heavy, as if she were weighed down by chains.

"You will accomplish nothing by forcing your case," Mrs. Summersby said. "It's not as if you have a contract. No constable will help you." She rapped on the roof. "We are on our own. Be rational, Lady Kerry."

The carriage jerked into movement, and Fontaine peered out the window at the departing building. As much as she didn't want to admit it, Mrs. Summersby was right. They had no leverage to force Mr. Newton into surrendering the children. Their agreement had hardly been within the law. She had no way to prove that he had taken her money. If she stormed inside, she would only anger him, and then he might refuse to let her take any other orphans in the future. Assuming he didn't call constables to take her away or report her actions to the foundation.

"I won't give up," Fontaine whispered.

Mrs. Summersby huffed. "Whoever said we were giving up? We are simply gathering reinforcements."

Fontaine turned to the woman. "You don't disapprove?"

Mrs. Summersby folded her hands in her lap. "I thought you were completely scandalous at first. I couldn't understand why you would risk so much for a group of children. But then…" She sighed. "Do you know that I almost did not accept my nieces and nephew when they were brought to my door?"

Fontaine shook her head. The proper, stern Mrs. Summersby didn't seem like the kind of woman who would get involved in the affairs of children who were not related to her by blood. It had been an odd choice for her to become their guardian, but Fontaine hadn't considered it to be any of her business when she'd learned of the baronet's death.

"What changed your mind?" Fontaine asked.

Mrs. Summersby's lips twisted. "I saw the fear in their faces and realized that they were as alone as I was. I thought that if we were together, I wouldn't feel the pain of my husband's loss so keenly." She sniffed. "So, you see, it was not for the children at all that I accepted them. It was for my own selfish reasons."

The pain in Mrs. Summersby's face, a mirror of Fontaine's

own, chased away all thought of the workhouse. She put her hand on the woman's knee. "You might feel that it was selfish, but I disagree."

Mrs. Summersby sniffed. "What do you mean?"

Fontaine nudged closer so her fabric-clad knees were pressed against Mrs. Summersby's. "You didn't want the children to fill a gap in your life. You felt what they felt. It would have been much easier for you to throw them out, but you didn't. You were young, and recently widowed."

Fontaine remembered the death of her own husband. Even if they had not been in love and had only married because her father had encouraged the match, Malcom's death had still hurt. They had been friends. She had struggled to find a sense of purpose after his death.

"Thank you," Mrs. Summersby whispered.

At that moment, Fontaine realized how close they were. Mrs. Summersby's soft cheek was inches from her lips. Their foreheads were nearly pressed together. A faint aroma of roses tangled in her nose. Here was a woman who knew exactly what Fontaine had felt.

Mrs. Summersby's cheeks were significantly pinker than they had been moments ago. Her lush lips were slightly parted, and a soft puff of air came from her lips and brushed against Fontaine's.

All she had to do was reach out and press their mouths together or slide her fingers into Mrs. Summersby's hair and draw her close. Their curves would press together in all the right places, and—she couldn't think of such things. Mrs. Summersby had shown no sign of returning Fontaine's interest. There had been no subtle touching, no fluttering of her eyelashes, no whispered invitations to take themselves somewhere more private.

Mrs. Summersby's eyes dilated. The tip of her tongue flicked across her lips.

Or had she merely overlooked the signs?

"Mrs. Summersby," she whispered. She moved her face fractionally closer.

"W-What is it?" Mrs. Summersby asked. She did not pull away but scooted even closer. The space between their lips was hardly more than the page of a book.

Fontaine's heart hammered in her chest, and a thrumming kind of tension passed through her, coalescing in that special spot between her thighs.

The carriage bounced, shattering the moment.

Chapter Nine

ROSEMARY WAS LIGHTHEADED from the force of the sensation pulsing through her. She had never shared a moment of such intensity with anyone. She had never known such feelings were *possible*. It left her scattered, but even in such a state, she knew they could not continue, and not simply because of their reputations. Lady Kerry seemed to care little about what society thought of her, as evidenced by her hosting the ladies' group, wearing bloomers, and venturing into Whitechapel.

She had intended to lecture Lady Kerry on the proper way for a titled woman to achieve one's ambitions—through careful maneuvering and manipulation, *not* direct action—but had ended up nearly swooning into the woman's arms. The change in plans left her rattled, uncertain what to do next. It was a very unpleasant feeling. She shoved her hands in her skirts and stared determinedly out the window. Only after several minutes had passed did she realize something was wrong. That bobbing light in the distance, barely visible through the fog that had settled over London. She'd seen it before. Several times, in fact.

"I believe we are being followed," she said.

"What?" Lady Kerry pressed herself to the window. "Who?"

Rosemary pointed to the light. "See that? It's been behind us since we left the workhouse."

Lady Kerry cursed like a sailor, making Rosemary gasp. It was easy to forget that the dowager baroness had not always been a lady, that she had started her life on the streets. She should have chastised her, but she felt a secret thrill. Was this how Saffron and Angelica had felt when they had engaged in their own adventures?

It was quite addictive.

"No need for concern," Rosemary said. "They won't be able to follow us for long. See?" She tapped on the window. "The traffic is as busy as ever."

"I can't see them anymore." Lady Kerry tilted her body back and forth. "Are they still out there?"

She shifted over. "Look from here."

Lady Kerry rose shakily to her feet and lurched across the small space to fall beside Rosemary. Unfortunately, the carriage was so tight that even with the other woman leaning toward the small circle of glass, their bodies were in close contact. She felt every inch of Lady Kerry's thigh and hip pressed against hers, despite the many layers separating them.

"Do you see it?" Rosemary asked. Her voice was raspier than it should have been, but Lady Kerry did not appear to notice.

"Yes," Lady Kerry said tightly.

"I suppose they might not be following us," Rosemary said, forcing herself to consider more reasonable possibilities. "It might be a coincidence."

"No, it's us they are after," Lady Kerry said. She leaned further out the window, giving Rosemary a lovely view of her rear. After more than a minute of staring, imagining what might lie beneath the soft layers of Lady Kerry's silk and cambric gown, Rosemary forced her gaze to her feet.

Lady Kerry hissed in a breath. "There's something on the door… A crest, I think."

"What does it look like?" Rosemary asked before almost smacking herself. There was no need to ask, as she could see for herself. She peered out her own window, but it was too late. Their pursuer had vanished.

"Do you think it was Mr. Newton?" Lady Kerry asked.

"Why would he follow us?" Rosemary asked, trying not to think about how Lady Kerry's waist and arm were tucked close to hers. If Rosemary adjusted her hand, she could twine their fingers together…

"Maybe it was the blackguards who have been kidnapping children from the street," Lady Kerry said. She bit her bottom lip. "My ship leaves tomorrow afternoon. How am I going to get the children out of the workhouse before then? The criminals might already have taken them."

Rosemary shoved her hand into her pocket before she could do something unwise. "As for that, I might have an idea."

A RAP AT her cottage door had Rosemary rising from her seat and wiping away the tears of mirth that had sprung at the corners of her eyes. Lady Kerry, it turned out, was an entertaining guest. Neither of them had mentioned what had happened in the carriage, which was perfectly fine with her. The less she thought about kissing Lady Kerry, the better.

When she entered the hallway, Nelly was already opening the door to several guests. There was her niece Saffron, wearing a very proper pink-and-cream day dress embroidered with white flowers. Saffron's husband, Leo, stepped into the cottage behind her, his hands shoved into his pockets. He was dressed in all black, as was his usual style, and had tied his long, golden hair back with a strip of leather. He flashed a rakish grin that would have sent many society ladies swooning but had no impact on Rosemary.

"Move, Leo," a feminine voice said. "Some of us would like to be out of the rain while the sun is still in the sky."

Leo took Saffron's elbow and stepped away from the door to reveal another pair of guests.

"Lord and Lady Lowell," Rosemary said, dipping into a curtsey. "It is an honor."

"I will have none of that formality," the raven-haired Marchioness of Lowell said, with a swish of her scarlet, cambric skirts. "It is 'Olivia,' for you, as always. Saffron described your situation in such terms that I could simply not resist joining. The Summersby family certainly gets into all manner of fantastic situations."

"We are here to assist," the Marquess of Lowell said as he stepped behind his wife and clasped his hands on her shoulders. "Forgive my wife, Mrs. Summersby. She sometimes forgets she is forbidden to seek adventure without me." His eyes twinkled, although she couldn't see much of his face beneath his wiry, black beard.

Rosemary's throat grew. She hadn't expected *all* of them to respond to her call for help.

"Glad to see you again, Thel," Leo said as he clasped arms with the marquess. The two men were nearly the same height, towering over everyone else in the room. Lord Lowell's hair was as dark, whereas Leo's was light, a pattern echoed in reverse in their suits.

"Likewise," Lord Lowell said with a grin. "You must bring Lily to visit Charmaine. My youngest daughter is nearly too much for her governess to handle without a playmate to tire her out."

"You can reacquaint yourselves later," Olivia said as she ushered the two men inside. They had to duck beneath a beam in the ceiling, and in doing so nudged a bookshelf full of figurines Rosemary's husband had given her throughout their three-year marriage. She lunged forward, arms outstretched, but Olivia beat her, catching a delicate, white ceramic fox in her palm before setting it back in place.

"Thank you," Rosemary said.

"Of course," Olivia said. Then she tugged off her glove and swatted her husband and Leo with it. "Brutes, the both of you! You must have more care in a lady's home."

They wore matching expressions of chagrin, like children having been reprimanded by their mother for coming home caked in mud. They reminded Rosemary so much of Basil. The boy had been a bundle of trouble, even drawing his sisters into his antics. She had struggled to contain their collective energy and had often resorted to convincing their governess to chase them up and down the stairs to tire them out.

The sound of footfalls drew Rosemary out of her bittersweet memories. She turned to find Lady Kerry standing in the entrance to the drawing room, her hands clasped at her waist.

Rosemary walked to stand beside the baroness and gestured toward the new arrivals. "Lord and Lady Lowell, and Lord and Lady Briarwood, may I introduce the Dowager Lady Kerry. Lady Kerry, it is my pleasure to introduce the Marquess and Marchioness of Lowell, and Viscount and Viscountess Briarwood."

Lady Kerry curtsied. "My lords, my ladies."

Lord Lowell snorted. "Don't 'lord' me. It's just 'Thel.'"

Rosemary sniffed. She was willing to accept that level of familiarity with Leo as her niece's husband, but not with Lord Lowell.

Lady Kerry rose from her curtsey with flushed cheeks.

Olivia placed her hand on her husband's arm. "We mustn't make Lady Kerry uncomfortable, my dear."

Lord Lowell bowed slightly. "My apologies. You can call me whatever you wish, Lady Kerry."

Leo flicked open the first button of his suit jacket. "Any friend of Rosemary's is a friend of mine. Tell us what you need, and we will help you."

Saffron stepped forward and took Lady Kerry's hands. "My husband is correct. I am very pleased to meet you."

Lady Kerry's eyes went so huge, she resembled an owl. "Y-Yes, of course. Thank you. I-I…"

The shine in Lady Kerry's eyes coupled with the way her throat worked made butterflies take wing in Rosemary's chest. She smiled at her guests. "Please take a seat. My maid will bring out refreshments."

Saffron and the men exited the room quickly, but Olivia remained for a moment longer. Her eyebrows lifted and lips quirked in a manner that made heat rise to Rosemary's cheeks. But before she could say anything, Olivia followed the others.

"Thank you," Lady Kerry whispered. Her face was splotched with red, and tears dripped down her cheeks. "We can save the children."

Presented with such emotion, Rosemary's words of reassurance vanished. Lady Kerry was so much like Saffron, caring more about others than herself. The two of them would make great friends.

Lady Kerry wiped her tears away with a flick of her wrist, then said in a much steadier voice. "Thank you, Mrs. Summersby."

"Of course," Rosemary whispered. She wanted to say more, to reassure Lady Kerry that everything would be fine, to draw the woman into her arms and—

Where had that thought come from? She had told Saffron she intended to convince Lady Kerry to consider more logical paths to accomplish her goals, not become emotionally involved.

"Are you sure you want to do this?" she asked.

"What alternative do we have?" Lady Kerry sighed. "I will not abandon Annie and the others."

"You could focus your attention somewhere else," Rosemary said. "Between Lord Lowell and Leo, we could—"

Lady Kerry shook her head. "No. Going through the proper channels would take too long. I have to leave for Halifax tomorrow and I... I know what it's like to be abandoned." She straightened. "We should join the others."

Rosemary obediently followed Lady Kerry to join the rest of the group, who were lounging around Rosemary's oak dining room table. Leo stretched his legs, but Lord Lowell was not so lucky. He sat with his knees coming nearly up to his waist. This earned a giggle from Saffron until Olivia swatted her.

"What manner of difficulty are we facing, then?" Olivia asked. "I do not want to remain away from home for too long."

Saffron touched her arm. "I understand. They are hard to leave at such a young age."

Olivia shook her head. "Between my stepdaughter, nieces, nephews, and now Charmaine, our house is so full of children, I can hardly descend a single set of stairs without tripping over some toy or bauble." But the glimmer in her eyes suggested this was not something that bothered her. Then she smiled at Lady Kerry. "I apologize for my impatience. Please, tell us what we can do to help."

"Oh, I understand completely," Lady Kerry said, all in a rush. She glanced at Rosemary, gulped, then continued. "You see, there is a, well, a business that I've been visiting for months using—I mean *acting* on behalf of the foundation, and…"

Lady Kerry's bumbling attempt at describing their problem in socially acceptable terms was both adorable and frustrating. Adorable because every time the baroness tripped over a word, she waved her hands around in increasingly frantic motions. Frustrating because this awkward Lady Kerry was entirely different from the confident woman who had spoken at the charity group, and they didn't have time to navigate such trivial issues as manners. So, when Lady Kerry paused, Rosemary said, "The Whitechapel workhouse is holding four orphans hostage."

Lady Kerry's jaw dropped open. Olivia squealed. Saffron gave a resigned sigh.

"I will spare you a description of the place." Rosemary shuddered. "You do not want to know the conditions those children are kept in. All you need to know is that Mr. Newton refuses to give them up."

"Can we not just pay the man?" Leo asked, reaching into his pocket. "If it is only a matter of money…"

"I tried that," Lady Kerry said. "He threw my money back at me. I believe someone is putting pressure on him." Her shoulders slumped. "As much as I don't want to believe the foundation is involved, I've proof that unrecorded children are being shipped to the foundation's branch in Halifax. It must be one of the city's gangs. I fear they are getting paid per child, much like the foundation pays me to secure orphans, although I have no idea why."

"Ah," Leo said. He cracked his neck. "We could track down the blackguards. It's been an age since I had a chance to fight."

"A fight?" Lord Lowell perked up.

Saffron put a hand on her husband's arm. "Absolutely not."

"We can sort out the mystery later," Rosemary said. "For now, we have to concentrate on getting the orphans away from the workhouse. You have a place to bring them, do you not, Lady Kerry?"

She was willing to play her part in the rescue, but she was not a nursemaid or a governess. She was not interested in revisiting her past and taking responsibility for children, especially ones who likely required far more care than she could provide. Basil's rebellious nature and eventual accidental death had proved that she lacked the tender touch required to be a proper guardian.

"The foundation keeps a well-guarded house by the docks," Lady Kerry said. "That is where the orphans we collect for the relocation scheme stay until they are deemed ready to make the journey to Halifax." She looked at her clasped hands on the table. "But Mr. Newton might not let them go easily."

"So, we break in and take them," Leo said.

Olivia grinned. "A midnight escapade? Yes, I would very much enjoy that."

"We will do what we can," Lord Lowell said. He met Leo's gaze, and the other man nodded.

"Ideas?" Leo asked. "How shall we retrieve these children without tipping off the fiendish Mr. Newton?"

Lady Kerry blinked rapidly. "You really mean to help?"

"Of course," Olivia said. "What did you expect? That is why we came."

Rosemary stepped closer to Lady Kerry, who seemed to be

on the brink of bursting into tears again. "Tell us what to do."

As if the words had flicked a toggle inside her, Lady Kerry's expression cleared. "Mr. Newton knows Mrs. Summersby and me, but if someone else were to distract them, we might be able to sneak in and retrieve the children." She paced the room. "We would need a large, and discreet, carriage. Perhaps two. And we'll have to wear clothing that won't slow us down."

"This is marvelous!" Olivia said. She bounced to her feet, raised her arms, and twirled. "For one night, we become common thieves."

Lord Lowell grasped his wife's hands in his own, then spun her into his arms and dipped her. The sight was terribly romantic and made Rosemary smile. She had rarely met a couple who were so open with their affection.

"We can use the Briarwood carriage," Saffron said. She took her husband's outstretched hand and rose unsteadily to her feet. "It is less conspicuous than that gold monstrosity of yours, Olivia."

Lord Lowell and Leo both laughed as they led their wives back to the entrance. Lady Kerry made several more attempts at thanking the assembled group, even following them outside. At last, it was only Rosemary and Saffron standing in the doorway.

"I was pleased when you told me you had made a friend in Lady Kerry," Saffron said. "But are you certain that is all this is?"

Her raised eyebrows made Rosemary wonder if she hadn't been as discreet in her previous relationships with women as she'd thought. But the lack of censure in her niece's voice was reassuring. She hadn't been sure how Saffron would react until that moment, nor had she understood how much relief it would give her to know Saffron didn't disapprove.

Rosemary swallowed past a lump in her throat and smiled. "We are friends, nothing more."

Even if she wished otherwise.

Chapter Ten

FONTAINE STOOD ON the banks of a muddy river behind the Whitechapel workhouse in the dead of night, breathing shallowly through her mouth. Lady Lowell and Mrs. Summersby waited beside her, their faces tinged faintly green. Only Lady Briarwood was missing, as her husband had forbidden her from joining them, owing to her current pregnancy. Fontaine studied Lady Lowell. The marchioness was nothing like the high-ranking members of her late father's circle. Those ladies and gentlemen had treated her like a curio, a thing to be gawked at when not carefully stored away. Perhaps that was why she'd fallen to pieces when Lord and Lady Lowell had been so sympathetic to her cause. She'd never had trouble entertaining a crowd, but her audiences rarely held titles higher than viscountess.

The rattle of wheels and whinny of horses sounded in the distance. Fontaine shifted her stance. The ground squelched beneath her feet.

"Is it almost time?" Lady Lowell asked. She plucked at the fabric of her skirt. "I fear I will have to burn this gown when we are done."

"Soon," Fontaine said. She still couldn't believe Mrs. Summersby had not only agreed to this impromptu rescue but had involved others. She owed Mrs. Summersby a debt and didn't know how she would repay it.

The screech of a whistle pierced the air, a signal they had

agreed upon with the men, who would cause a distraction at the front of the workhouse while they snuck in through the back.

She pushed through the muck to the door she had snuck out countless times as a child. None of the other orphans in the workhouse had used it, fearing they would be discovered by mud stains on their boots. She had been the only child willing to risk beatings for brief moments of freedom.

Choosing this entry point had been a calculated risk, but she felt confident that Mr. Newton would not have fixed it after taking ownership of the workhouse, even after so many years, and her guess was proven correct as she placed a palm on the door and it creaked open.

She exhaled slowly, emitting a large cloud of mist that vanished into the smoggy air above them. "Let's go."

They entered the chilly, dimly lit house and crept down a narrow hallway toward a rectangle of light: the entrance to the kitchen. When they reached it, she held up a hand to instruct the others to stop, then peered around the doorframe. There were three elderly women inside the kitchen, but all of them had their backs to her. She waved Lady Lowell and Mrs. Summersby past her, then darted across.

The floorboards gave a faint creak with each step, but she could barely hear it over the pounding of her own pulse in her ears. When they reached the stairs, the sound of voices approaching had them freezing in place.

"Go," Lady Lowell whispered. "I'll take care of it."

Fontaine hesitated for only a moment before taking Mrs. Summersby's hand and rushing up the stairs. The children would be in a different room than the one they had seen on their last trip. That room was used during inspections. At all other times, the orphans slept in the attic. They would remain there all hours of the day when they were not working, not leaving even for fresh air or exercise.

Mrs. Summersby squeezed her hand as they approached the room. It was locked, but Fontaine knew the trick of the door, having forced it open many times. She pulled a piece of twisted wire from her pocket and stuck it in the keyway. A jerk of her wrist was all it took, and the lock clicked open.

"Wait here," she told Mrs. Summersby. "They might need convincing."

The other woman looked as if she were going to argue, but then she heaved a sigh and nodded. "Be quick."

When Fontaine entered, the smell that greeted her was even worse than before. The children inside lay on the floor, clutching each other and shivering in the darkness. The only light came from the dingy windows, which were nailed shut and lacking curtains or blinds.

One child stood and moved toward them. "You came back."

It was Annie, sporting a large bruise on her cheek. As Fontaine stepped forward, Annie cringed.

"I'm sorry," Fontaine whispered.

Annie touched the bruise on her face with her fingertips. "Did you come to take us away?"

"Yes."

The other children huddled closer together, whispering words she couldn't quite make out. She understood their fear, their reluctance to trade their awful, but known, situation for one that might be even worse.

"I know you don't trust me," she said. "But if we don't leave now, I don't know what will happen to you." She crouched down so her head was level with the girl. "I was living 'ere, 'afore the place was owned by a toff."

All the children gasped.

"Were you really?" Annie asked.

Fontaine pointed to a corner of the room. "Check over there. I carved my name into the wall."

Annie narrowed her eyes but walked to where Fontaine had pointed.

"Frannie," Fontaine said. "That's me."

She remembered getting on her hands and knees and carving

her name, a few scratches at a time, using a nail she had pried out of the floor. She had feared her own death was imminent and had wanted to ensure that some part of her remained, even if it was only a series of rough marks made by her own hand.

Annie returned to stand between Fontaine and the others. "That proves nothing."

At that moment, Fontaine realized there was someone else in the room, a slim figure tucked beneath several blankets in the corner.

"No!" a new voice cried as Fontaine walked toward the shape.

When she was close enough to make out the child, her throat grew thick. The poor creature was little more than skin and bones. His damp hair stuck to his head above his wide, cloudy eyes.

"You don't want him," Peter said, shoving himself between her and the mattress. "He's too sick to do you any good."

The fear shining out of his face made her want to drop to her knees and wrap her arms around him, but that would only elicit more fear.

"I can help him," she said.

The boy's face held a mix of hope and fear. She knew how he felt. It was difficult to trust when you had been let down so many times. She had to show him she meant well.

"I'll make sure you aren't separated," she said. "But we have to get out of here right now."

His eyes filled with tears. "Do you promise?"

She nodded, although part of her wondered how they were going to get a sick child out of the building without being caught.

"We have to go," Mrs. Summersby whispered.

Fontaine jumped. She had been so focused on the orphans that she hadn't noticed the other woman entering.

"Take the others," Fontaine said. "I'll stay with Peter and..." She looked at the boy on the ground.

"Quinn," Peter said. "My twin brother's name is Quinn."

"Don't do this," Mrs. Summersby whispered. "Those two will only slow us down."

"It doesn't matter," Fontaine said. She knew what it was like to be left, how heartbreaking it was to watch her friends disappear one by one. She would not inflict that upon another child if she had any other choice. She had seen enough death in her time to recognize when it was near. By her estimation, Quinn would be dead before the week's end.

Mrs. Summersby huffed. "You leave me no choice." Then she grabbed Fontaine's upper arm and wrenched her toward the door.

"No!" Fontaine shouted. "I can carry him!" Even though Mrs. Summersby was right. Quinn would get them caught. She struggled, but Mrs. Summersby was stronger than she appeared.

"It's too much of a risk," Mrs. Summersby said softly. "We have to get the rest of them to safety first." She turned to Annie and the others. "If the rest of you want to live, follow me."

Then the children mobbed them, and it was too late. She couldn't fight off Mrs. Summersby without risking hurting a child. As they exited the room, she turned her head, catching one last glimpse of Peter standing beside his brother, his arms at his side, his expression twisted in betrayal.

She wanted to scream, to force the children that clung to her skirts away and claw her way back, but she knew she couldn't. She swallowed her anger, forcing her mind to the challenge still in front of them: escaping the workhouse without being caught.

They slunk through the twisting hallways of the building, using routes she knew from her time as a resident were the least used. They had made it to the main floor when she heard shouting and banging. Hopefully, that meant their distraction was working. She would owe Lord Lowell and Lord Briarwood a boon for their part in assisting her.

"We're almost there," Fontaine whispered. Then she bumped into someone and nearly screamed. Thankfully, she recognized Lady Lowell at the last second and clenched her jaw shut.

"There you are," Mrs. Summersby said. "Lady Kerry, take the children. We'll watch from here."

Fontaine ushered the orphans on, but when she glanced over her shoulder, Mrs. Summersby was whispering something to Lady Lowell. The other woman nodded, then rushed off in the other direction. Fontaine didn't have time to ponder the implications of the interaction because in the next second, they reached the kitchen. She gestured to the children to press their backs along the wall, then peeked around the edge.

A wave of cold washed over her. More than a dozen women stood inside, some close enough to the door frame to snatch a child trying to pass. It was too dangerous. They would have to find a different route out of the house.

"What was that?" a voice from inside the kitchen asked.

Fontaine pressed herself as close to the wall as she could. One of the kitchen workers stood with her back to the door, so close that Fontaine could make out the deep wrinkles on her face. If the woman merely turned her head, she would see them.

Fontaine didn't dare move, lest the creak of the floor alert them. She imagined herself becoming one with the wallpaper behind her, breathing in through her nose and out through her mouth, praying none of the children would sneeze or let out a cry. After a full minute had elapsed, she risked turning her head and found Mrs. Summersby had clasped her hands over the mouths of two of the children, and the others were covering their mouths themselves. The eyes of all of them were wide and bright with fear.

Fontaine met Mrs. Summersby's gaze, and something electric passed between them, shooting straight from Fontaine's chest to her toes. Time passed slowly, each heartbeat echoing in her head. Then a loud thump sounded above them, and several women inside the kitchen began speaking at once.

"What was that?"

"The children!"

"It must be Annie again."

The woman standing in the doorway vanished.

Fontaine peeled herself away from the wall and ushered the children down the hall, one at a time, until the adults were the only ones left.

A shouting from deeper in the house had the kitchen workers standing about. Fontaine had no hope of waiting for them to settle back down, and she couldn't stay where she was, or risk being caught. After a quick prayer for luck, she lifted her skirts and dashed across the gap. The women inside cried out, and the sound of pots banging and knives being dropped followed.

"Run!" Fontaine shouted.

They raced down the hallway, then flew out the door onto the riverbank. Fontaine was the last, and when she closed the door behind her, she grabbed the shaved chunk of wood she had saved for this purpose and shoved it beneath the door from the outside. It would not delay their pursuers for long, but hopefully, they could escape without being followed.

The sucking mud slowed their progress, and the children were tired and exhausted, but in a matter of minutes, they had made it through the muck and shoved the children into the carriage Lord Briarwood had arranged. Not a moment too late, as the door to the workhouse burst open, and Mr. Newton stood in the doorway, looking furious.

Fontaine slammed the door of the carriage shut and settled herself with the children, who were shivering and holding each other. It was a good thing they had brought the largest carriage that any of the adults had possessed, or they might not have had room for all of them.

They sat in silence as the carriage moved through the streets. Fontaine clutched Mrs. Summersby's hand, heaving cold air into her lungs. She had to see the children safely to the foundation's staging home. Then they would be safe.

"You shouldn't have tried to stay behind," Mrs. Summersby said.

Fontaine stared at her. "What?"

Mrs. Summersby pressed her lips together. "You could've been caught."

Fontaine shook her head. "You don't understand."

Before her father had found her, there had been several incidents when a family would come to the workhouse seeking a child to adopt. Then, when someone else had been selected, she'd been filled with bitter jealousy and disappointment.

Mrs. Summersby sighed. "You cannot continue to risk yourself. If you keep doing this, there will be a time when you will lose everything."

The children watched the exchange with wide eyes, probably unused to being in such fine transport.

The carriage turned a corner and slowed.

"What's going—" Fontaine started to ask before the door opened and two figures crawled inside the cramped carriage: Lady Lowell and Peter.

"There you are," Mrs. Summersby said. "I was beginning to worry."

Lady Lowell threw back her hood and grinned. "How could you ever doubt me?"

Then Fontaine noticed Lady Lowell holding a small, blanket-clad shape in her arms.

Quinn.

"You sent Lady Lowell back for them," Fontaine said, her voice breaking.

"Isn't that what you said?" Mrs. Summersby said brusquely. "We do not leave any behind."

It took every ounce of Fontaine's willpower not to kiss her.

Chapter Eleven

ROSEMARY WAITED IN the carriage as Lady Kerry ran through the sheeting rain to pound on the door of a nondescript brick building. With so many bodies cramped in a small space, it quickly warmed, although Quinn still trembled in Olivia's arms. Peter sat so close to his brother that Olivia essentially had both boys on her lap.

Annie threaded her fingers through Rosemary's. "You won't leave us here, will you?"

The question slipped between Rosemary's ribs and plunged into her heart.

"You could let us go," Annie continued. "We'll be fine on our own. The boys just need some fresh air and they'll be all right."

Before Rosemary could come up with some manner of placating response that wouldn't make her feel guiltier than she already did, she glimpsed something in Annie's eyes. It was subtle, but Rosemary had helped raise three precocious children and recognized scheming when she saw it.

"Clever," Rosemary said, squeezing her fingers around Annie's before pulling away.

Annie rolled her eyes. "That usually works with adults."

Rosemary nudged Annie's shoulder with her own. "I'm not like most adults."

The girl grumbled and crossed her arms.

A creak signaled the opening of the door, and the children

leaned away as Lady Kerry entered, looking like she had dragged herself out of the river, both from the sodden state of her cloak and the lack of color in her face.

"They're full," Lady Kerry said. She shoved into her seat beside Rosemary, causing the carriage to rock slightly. Some of the damp from Lady Kerry's cloak soaked into Rosemary's dress. Rather than complain, she gathered her skirts and tucked them beneath her legs.

"Where do we take them, then?" Olivia asked.

"You could let us go," Annie said. "We're used to sleeping on the streets. We'll find a place."

"No!" Peter cried. He flung his body over his brother. "It's fine for you, Annie, but Quinn isn't strong enough."

"Oh," Annie said, shrinking in her seat. "Sorry, Peter. I forgot about Quinn."

Olivia gently pushed Peter off her lap. "We will not return you to the streets, darling. There must be some other option."

"My townhouse," Lady Kerry said. "It's not ideal, but it will have to do." She wiped droplets of water from her face with the back of her hand, although Rosemary could not tell if it was tears or the rain.

Then Lady Kerry exited the carriage again, presumably to tell the driver their new location, although she could have done so without braving the rain a second time.

"This has exceeded even my lofty expectations," Olivia said as she shuffled the shivering bundle in her arms. "Do you think she regularly hosts groups of orphans? I admit, I've never considered the possibility."

"We're much better company than fancy ladies and gents," Annie said. "We'll even help with the chores, won't we, boys?"

Peter mumbled something as he stared at his brother. Xavier stared determinedly out the window. Winter picked at a loose thread in a blanket.

The thought of the children running around Lady Kerry's home dressed in servants' livery was both amusing and sobering.

The sad truth was, unless they were lucky enough to be adopted or find employment, they might never escape living on the street. Even the few who were adopted might still perish before they reached adulthood from cholera or tuberculosis.

Lady Kerry's foundation was trying to do good by sending orphans across the ocean, but as the baroness re-entered the carriage, Rosemary wondered if Halifax was really so different a fate for these children than London.

ANNIE CLUTCHED ROSEMARY'S hand as they ascended the narrow, carpeted staircase to the second floor of Lady Kerry's townhouse behind Olivia. There were no paintings decorating the walls, no lavish pieces of furniture crowding the entryway, no servants bustling about. It was as if they had entered the ghost of a home. Even the children, who had yammered away like magpies in the carriage, were silent.

They walked down a dark hall and came to a door, which Lady Kerry opened. Ten metal-framed beds filled the space, each holding a gray blanket and a small pillow.

"I keep a small staff," Fontaine said, as if sensing Rosemary's confusion. "My lady's maid, Jones, recently left to be married, and I have not yet replaced her."

They walked down a dark hall and came to a door, which Lady Kerry opened. A huge, four-poster bed filled the room, along with a dressing table, chair, and several other pieces of sturdy-looking furniture.

"There are several guest rooms on this floor," Lady Kerry said. "You can take whichever you want.

Annie released Rosemary's hand and ran down the hallway squealing, followed by a much more stoic Xavier. Peter followed Olivia like a chick as she deposited her bundle on the bed. He then joined his brother and lay beside him.

"Lady Lowell—" Lady Kerry said before the other woman shushed her and crawled onto the bed with the two boys, clutching them to her sides like a mother hen. The sight was enough to make Rosemary's throat grow thick as she remembered the time Angelica had come down with a fever and Rosemary had caught both Basil and Saffron out of their beds long after midnight, cuddled together in the same position.

Time passed so quickly. It felt like yesterday that she'd been the guardian of her nieces and nephew, and now Basil was gone, and both Angelica and Saffron were happily married.

There was nothing left for Rosemary to do.

"Let's leave them," Lady Kerry whispered. "I'll send for the foundation's physician."

They stepped out of the room and Lady Kerry closed the door softly.

Rosemary should have murmured the appropriate words, stepped away, and returned to her home. She had done exactly what she'd told Lady Kerry she would do. But the combination of Lady Kerry's lost expression and the way she had her arms wrapped around herself spoke of vulnerability.

Rosemary shouldn't have cared. She had been very careful to avoid forming emotional attachments since living on her own. Once one started down the path of worrying about people who were none of one's concern, it was difficult to stop. She'd seen Saffron lose herself in anxiety too many times to make that mistake. At the same time, she'd experienced enough lonely nights to make it difficult to walk away from Lady Kerry when she looked so despondent.

"Will Quinn…" Rosemary's voice was tight. She cleared her throat and tried again, whispering so the children would not hear. "Do you think Quinn will survive?"

Lady Kerry sighed, and at that moment, she seemed a decade older. Like a woman who had lived through all the horror and injustice the world had to offer but refused to let it break her.

"I see," Rosemary said. She forced her eyes wide to keep back the tears that threatened to burst free. It didn't matter that they had gone to such great lengths to free Quinn and the others from the workhouse. Children died every day. There was no reason for Rosemary to become overcome with emotion.

Lady Kerry removed a handkerchief from her pocket and dabbed at her damp cheeks. "The foundation will do everything possible for Quinn."

After a tense moment, in which Rosemary wasn't sure if she should offer sympathy or change the topic, Lady Kerry shoved her handkerchief back into her pocket and lifted her chin. "It's too late to find somewhere else to take them, and Mr. Newton might reclaim them if they return to the streets." Her lower lip trembled. "I have no choice. I can't leave."

Unfamiliar sensations stirred in Rosemary's chest. Even though Lady Kerry's insistence on doing everything herself was absurd, Rosemary had to admire her dedication. She had opened her home to orphans just as Rosemary had accepted her nieces and nephew. They were more similar than Rosemary wanted to admit. For that reason, she knew she couldn't leave Lady Kerry on her own.

Saffron's words from the previous day returned. Her niece had so casually dismissed the idea of her aunt engaging in anything exciting. Perhaps that was Rosemary's problem. She was always so careful, unwilling to risk experiencing the same hurt she'd seen her nieces suffer through, no matter the cost of her caution.

Perhaps it was time for that to change.

Chapter Twelve

AS FONTAINE ESCORTED Mrs. Summersby back to the front door, it felt as if her corset were far too tight. Each breath ended on a gasp and her vision darkened at the edges.

There were five—possibly four by morning—children in her house who had to be cared for, and nowhere to take them. The orphanages were full. What if she asked Captain Charles to allow her to bring the children with her to Halifax? That would get them out of Mr. Newton's reach, although she didn't know what she would do with them when they arrived, if the Halifax branch would take them in. Not to mention the difficult matter of feeding and supervising so many children along the journey.

She was getting ahead of herself. The captain likely wouldn't even allow her on board unless she brought along her supposed companion, especially if she had several children in tow. She shoved her hand into her pocket, seeking the one item she never left her house without. It was an awkward, and admittedly ironic, quirk of her past life that she still felt compelled to carry a box of matches with her everywhere. When she was nervous or anxious it calmed her to turn the small item around in her fingers.

"I'll come with you," Mrs. Summersby said. "You can hire someone to watch over the children or bring them with us."

Could she bribe the captain? Mr. Newton had initially refused her requests to take orphans from the workhouse until she had laid bills in his palm. That was the way of the world in Whitechapel, but she didn't know if the same rules held for sailors.

"Lady Kerry, did you hear what I said?"

Fontaine's legs wobbled. Finding Captain Charles had been a stroke of good luck. What were the odds that she could find another ship departing in the coming days for Halifax, especially one that would allow her to travel unaccompanied with a gaggle of children? If she did not sort out the problem with the foundation, Mrs. Eris would certainly report the problem to Mr. Hill, and then her chance of securing his endorsement would vanish. She would be removed from the board and would have to start again with a new charitable organization—assuming Mr. Hill didn't sour her reputation.

She put one hand on the wall and clamped down on the wiggling, unpleasant feelings in her stomach.

"Lady Kerry!"

Fontaine jerked her neck up to find Mrs. Summersby's nose inches from hers. The other woman's eyes were wide, her cheeks rosy, her lips slightly parted.

All thought of the children, and the foundation, vanished from Fontaine's mind. She had never noticed before, but Mrs. Summersby had two different-colored eyes. One was a dark blue, and the other was brown. There were also faint freckles spattered across the bridge of her nose, and a thin scar at her temple.

Fontaine raised her hand and touched the jagged section of raised skin. "How did you get this?"

The tip of Mrs. Summersby's tongue swept across her lips. "My nephew. Basil. I was carrying him down the steps and..." Her eyelids fluttered closed. "I fell."

Fontaine slid her hand down Mrs. Summersby's face, then curled her fingers about the other woman's neck. It would be so easy to kiss her. All she had to do was pretend to stumble, lean forward, brush their mouths together. If Mrs. Summersby recoiled, Fontaine could pretend it had been an accident and apologize.

She could do it. She *should* do it. What was the worst that could happen?

An image of Mrs. Summersby's face twisted into a mask of disgust appeared in her mind, before Fontaine banished it. Yes, there was the risk that Mrs. Summersby would reject her, but there was also the possibility of so much more. She imagined stoking Mrs. Summersby to a conflagration, bringing her pleasure over and over again until they were both boneless with exertion.

After everything she had lived through, she refused to let fear stop her from pursuing something she wanted.

She exhaled harshly through her nostrils and pressed fractionally closer until her chest was brushing Mrs. Summersby's.

"Can I kiss you?" Fontaine whispered.

The seconds seemed to pass like minutes as she waited for a reply, certain Mrs. Summersby would shove her away, then storm off in disgust. But when her response finally came, it was in the form of a whisper that caused gooseflesh to erupt on her arms.

"Yes."

They moved in unison, touching their lips together in the gentlest of caresses that sent waves of heat through Fontaine's body and made her long for more.

The noises Mrs. Summersby uttered did not help. She sounded as if they were already naked and tangled together on a bed, rather than touching in only one small place.

If a simple kiss was so powerful, what would it be like to taste the rest of Mrs. Summersby?

Fontaine increased the force of the kiss, just enough so that Mrs. Summersby knew it hadn't been a mistake. When she didn't pull away, Fontaine felt as if she would swoon right there. She had never felt this way with Malcom. This tense feeling, as if she were a balloon and at any moment, someone would prick her, and she would explode into a thousand pieces.

She wanted to slide her hands up Mrs. Fontaine's thighs, kiss every hollow on her body, taste the inside of her mouth and every other place she would allow her to taste.

Was it her imagination, or was Mrs. Summersby leaning in closer, too?

Then a hand touched her waist, and she gasped. The moment her lips parted, Mrs. Summersby's tongue swept inside hers, and the heat inside her increased tenfold.

Mrs. Summersby returned every stroke in equal measure. She raised her hand to Mrs. Summersby's breasts. A cry came from deep in her throat, which Fontaine eagerly swallowed, delving deep into the other woman's mouth while curling her arms about her back, drawing them so close that their stomachs pressed together.

Then the sound of distant carriage wheels filtered into her mind, and she realized they were on the brink of being discovered. She didn't want to pull back. She would rather have locked the door and crawled beneath Mrs. Summersby's skirts on the carpet before the fire. But Mrs. Summersby did not deserve their privacy to be interrupted in such a way.

She gentled her kisses, withdrawing slowly until they were once again panting with their foreheads touching. Mrs. Summersby's lips were swollen, her eyes cloudy, her cheeks rosy. A strand of silver hair had separated from her chignon and bobbed by her cheek.

It was the most beautiful thing Fontaine had ever seen.

"Lady Kerry, I..." Mrs. Summersby whispered. "I...haven't the faintest idea what to say."

"Call me 'Fontaine.'"

Mrs. Summersby licked her lips again, then said in a voice full of passion, "*Fontaine.*"

Was it too soon to kiss her again? The way the woman said her name, as if they were lovers, made her want to wrap her arms around Mrs. Summersby and whisk them to a bed. Preferably for the rest of the night, if not longer.

Mrs. Summersby tightened her fingers on Fontaine's waist. "I suppose you may have my leave to call me 'Rosemary.' Given the circumstances."

"I would very much like to kiss you again, Rosemary," Fontaine said.

Rosemary's cheeks somehow became even redder. She tilted her chin up. "I-I would like that as well. But… we cannot." She cleared her throat. "It wouldn't be proper. Not here."

Proper.

Of course, that was what she would say.

Unfortunately, she was very much correct. If they were discovered, their reputations would be ruined. They would be expelled from society, forced to live on the fringes, never truly accepted by their peers. Fontaine knew several such couples, and although they had never complained to her about their exile, she often wondered if they regretted making their relationship public.

"You are right," she said, as she leaned in. "We cannot."

"We absolutely can't," Rosemary replied.

They inched closer, noses brushing, breaths mingling, until Fontaine could see a smattering of faint freckles along Rosemary's cheeks. She was even more beautiful up close, wrinkles and all. Fontaine had always assumed that the stories she'd read about infatuation were elaborate lies designed to make marriage more bearable. She hadn't imagined that another woman could set her skin aflame, and make her nipples so erect, they dug into the material of her shift and corset.

"Once more," Fontaine whispered. "No one has to know."

Their lips touched, and she pressed herself to Rosemary, sliding her hands up the other woman's shoulders until her hands touched her hair. Then Rosemary was touching her back, and all sense of caution and rationality vanished from her mind. Every touch, even through so many layers, was scalding.

She removed her gloves, then brushed her fingers over Rosemary's bare throat, tracing the gentle lines until she reached her pulse, which thundered fiercely. She pressed an open-mouthed kiss to the spot. Rosemary gasped and threaded her fingers in Fontaine's hair.

Fontaine blew on the place where she had licked.

"Oh, stop that," Rosemary said.

Fontaine nibbled the spot where Rosemary's pulse felt strongest. "I don't want to stop."

"Neither do I, but we must."

Rosemary was right. They couldn't be together, and not just because society would scorn them. If anyone saw them together and told Mr. Hill, she would lose her post. She had her widow's portion, but it wasn't nearly enough to support her and continue her charitable efforts. She needed her place in society, her ability to move among the elite, in order to raise the funds, she required.

God, how she wished things were different. If they were both wealthy. If she didn't need to maintain her reputation. They could escape into the country and live together. But she couldn't simply turn her head and forget everything she had seen and lived through. The children of London needed her.

"Thank you for your assistance, Mrs. Summersby," Fontaine said, stepping back. "I could not have rescued the children without you."

Rosemary huffed. "Do you think I would allow you to continue this foolish quest of yours alone?" She pushed away from the wall and fluffed her skirts. "I will need time to pack. How long is the journey to Halifax?"

Fontaine's mouth dried. She couldn't believe what she was hearing. "You'll come with me?"

Rosemary flitted her hands over her hair, tucking strands back into place. "I already told you I would."

It should not have been such a surprise, after everything Rosemary had done in the past two days. She presented a stern, cold mask to the world, but in truth, she was the kindest and most generous person Fontaine had ever met.

"Thank you," Fontaine whispered thickly.

"Thank me when we have completed our task," Rosemary said as she opened the front door. But before she left, she cast a glance over her shoulder. That moment of eye contact, so full of promise, caused gooseflesh to erupt on Fontaine's arms.

Then Rosemary was gone, and Fontaine realized with a muttered curse that she'd just agreed to spend three weeks in close contact with a woman who could arouse her desires with a mere look.

Chapter Thirteen

R OSEMARY USHERED ANNIE down the dock, the soles of her shoes slapping on the damp planks. The cool, foggy night had given way to a blazing, afternoon sun, causing her to regret choosing her sturdiest walking suit made of scarlet corduroy for the first day of their journey. Between the oppressive heat and the tight clasp of the fabric around her body, she felt nearly as ready to leap out of her clothes as she had when Lady Kerry...*Fontaine*...had slipped her tongue inside Rosemary's mouth. Leaving that house had taken every ounce of willpower she'd possessed, and even then, she'd returned to her bed to bring herself to orgasm a dozen times before the conflagration that Fontaine had sparked inside her had ebbed.

She was out of her mind to be joining the dowager baroness on a journey across the ocean. There would be no avoiding each other. She would have to force her embarrassing infatuation away, bury it so deep that even Fontaine's winning smile and expressive eyes wouldn't revive it. She wouldn't allow herself to remember the warmth of Fontaine's hands caressing her neck and the faint taste of mint on her lips...

"Is that it?" Annie asked.

Rosemary shoved her lustful thoughts to the side and followed Annie's raised finger to the enormous ship looming at the end of the dock. Its black-painted iron hull contrasted against the bright-blue sky. Waves washed against its side, spraying sea foam that settled like a mist over their feet. Even without the billowing sails drawn, she felt a shiver of unease. She had only ever boarded small boats, the kind that went down rivers or across lakes. This ship, the S.S. *Great Arcadia*, was enormous in comparison.

Annie adjusted the brown, burlap sack slung over her shoulder and sidled closer. From the moment Rosemary had arrived at Fontaine's home that morning, Annie had clung to her like a chick. As much as she knew she had to sever the attachment Annie had formed—the girl would be staying in Halifax, Rosemary would not—it was difficult to push her away. Annie reminded her too much of Angelica, who had been similarly both shy and precocious at the same age.

Rosemary reached down and took Annie's hand. "Shall we try to get ahead of the others? Then we can have the first choice of beds."

Annie glanced at the line of passengers waiting to board ahead of them, then strode ahead much faster than before. In moments, they had caught up to the other children, all carrying burlap sacks stuffed with their few possessions. Fontaine stood in the middle of the pack, wearing a dark-green walking suit and holding a blanket-wrapped Quinn in her arms. The boy no longer trembled, but his face was pale and beaded with moisture.

"I couldn't leave him," Fontaine said. "The doctor said it's not cholera, but an infection."

Peter, standing beside Fontaine, reached up and tucked the blanket more securely around his brother. "He needs rest and food. Then he'll get stronger."

"Let me," Rosemary said, gesturing to Quinn. "You must be tired from holding him."

Fontaine's eyebrows shot up to her hairline. "Are you sure?" She looked down at Quinn, then back at Rosemary. "I didn't think you were..." Rather than complete the sentence, she shrugged, as if apologizing.

"Not fond of children?" Rosemary asked. She shook her head. "It has been some time, but when I took in my nieces and nephew, they were five, six, and ten-and-three."

She fondly remembered the chaos of that first month. Even though her parents had trained her to be a proper wife, she had not expected to go from a newly widowed, childless woman to a guardian of three in a matter of months. After the initial few days of shyness, Basil, Angelica, and Saffron had turned into terrible nuisances, or so she'd thought at the time. With the clarity of foresight, it was obvious that grief had steered her behavior. She had only wanted the best for them, but her frustration had manifested in a short temper. Deep down, she knew it was her fault that Basil had rebelled. Had she treated him kindlier, listened to his fears, he would not have felt the need to strike out on his own. If she'd been more like Fontaine, perhaps her nephew might have still been alive.

She wordlessly reached out her arms and accepted the blanket-wrapped bundle. As Fontaine stepped away, Rosemary hissed in a breath. Quinn was so light. She clutched the boy as tightly as she dared. This time, she vowed, she would not make the same mistake as she had with Basil. She would hold on to her temper with everything she had, no matter how often her patience was tested. The orphans had experienced enough cruelty to last them a lifetime.

"What do you plan to tell the captain?" Rosemary asked.

Before they had left Fontaine's townhouse, she had admitted that she had only negotiated passage for two.

"I won't tell him anything," Fontaine said. Then she crouched and drew the other children close. "Have all of you played tag behind before?"

"Of course," Peter said. He adjusted her sack on his shoulder. "But what about Quinn? He'll draw too much attention."

"We could nick a sack and carry him in that way," Annie said.

Rosemary stood outside the circle Fontaine had formed with the children, feeling as if she had been thrust from the planning, the only member of their party who had not lived on the street. But at the alarming mention of shoving frail Quinn into a bag, she leaned down. "Please tell me you have a plan."

Fontaine pushed to her feet. "I had intended to have the children find large families and follow behind them. It is a tactic street urchins often use to gain entrance to places they would not otherwise be allowed. They only need to hide until I can speak to Captain Charles."

Before Rosemary could protest this haphazard plan, the crowd pushed them forward, and the narrow dock made it impossible for the children to disperse.

"We'll have to convince the captain some other way," Fontaine said, her voice strained. Then she looked over her shoulder and paled. "Oh, no."

"What is it?" Rosemary asked. She followed Fontaine's gaze to a black carriage at the end of the dock. Etched on the door was the crest of a rearing lion.

"Is that the same one that followed us?" Rosemary asked.

"I'm not sure," Fontaine said. "I only saw it for a moment."

The door to the carriage opened, but the crowd moved before Rosmary could see who had exited.

"Lady Kerry, is that you?"

Rosemary straightened as a man wearing a bright-blue suit and a wide smile maneuvered through the crowd toward them.

"Mr. Eris," Fontaine said in a tight voice. "What are you doing here?"

"Traveling to Halifax, of course," the man asked. "Are you also traveling on foundation business?"

Rosemary realized with a start that the children had distanced themselves, as if realizing their presence might raise questions. That, or they feared strangers. Probably both.

"Who is this, then?" Mr. Eris asked, turning to Rosemary.

"M-My companion, Mrs. Summersby," Fontaine said. "We are to assess the progress of the relocation scheme."

Out of the corner of her eye, Rosemary spotted someone shoving through the crowd, causing a disturbance. She elbowed Fontaine in the ribs.

The dowager baroness gave an exaggerated swoon.

"Lady Kerry!" Mr. Eris cried. He reached for her. "Whatever is the matter?"

"The heat," Fontaine whispered. She waved her hand in front of her face. "It feels as if I have been standing in the sun for hours."

Mr. Eris huffed. "These ocean liners never consider the well-being of passengers. Well, the least I can do is offer you a faster embarkation." He winked. "Foundation privilege, eh?"

"We would not want to be a bother," Fontaine said, while taking his arm.

"Nonsense," Mr. Eris said. "Where is your luggage?"

"Our driver left them with the rest." Fontaine gestured toward the other end of the dock, where piles of trunks and bags were guarded by several sailors.

"Wait here a moment," Mr. Eris said. Then he squirmed through the crowd and spoke to a stern-faced sailor some distance ahead of them. When he returned, the sailor led them through the crowd, with Rosemary following behind. She worried at first what Mr. Eris would say when the children joined them, but he soon split off from them to join the first-class line, giving a wave before turning away.

Then she was standing in front of a tall, bald man with a winding snake tattooed across his bulging forearm.

"Tickets," he said.

"It's me, Cookie," Fontaine said. "Captain Charles agreed to transport my companion and me to Halifax."

Rosemary felt herself scowl. Who was this man to whom Fontaine referred by such a cute name?

The man squinted. "Who?" He reached into the pocket of his trousers and retrieved a pair of wire-rimmed spectacles, which he settled on his face. Then his scowl transformed into a wide smile. "Lady Kerry! I thought you might not make it." He tilted his head. "Who're them?"

The children clustered closer to the adults.

"Don't worry," Rosemary whispered to Xavier and Annie, hiding behind her. "Lady Kerry won't let them turn us away."

Fontaine stepped forward and clutched her hands together, as if praying. "Cookie, you must understand. These orphans have nowhere else to—"

"Orphans!" Cookie shouted. "Why didn't you say so? Bring 'em aboard. I'll see if I can find you another room."

"Ah, yes, thank you," Fontaine said. She met Rosemary's gaze, gave a helpless shrug, then ushered the children forward. The gigantic man reached down and lifted each of the children by the waist and onto the ship, making them squeal. Up close, Rosemary could see that one of the man's eyes was milky white, and the other a startling green. He grinned, displaying several gold teeth.

Rosemary stepped through the porthole without help but then danced on her feet with the rocking of the ship. Her stomach was already gurgling, which did not bode well for the rest of the journey. She kept one hand on the wall as they followed Cookie through the narrow halls of the ship. By the time he stopped at a closed door and removed a ring of keys from his belt, she was certain she would spend the entire journey leaning over the railing. How did one get used to the constant movement? She already missed the firm stillness of the earth beneath her feet.

Cookie unlocked the door and pushed it open, eliciting a series of gasps and squeals from the children.

Annie and Xavier were the first inside, shouting as they rushed inside. There were just enough beds for the children, and a single porthole that let in a small amount of light, interspersed with splashes of water.

"This is wonderful," Fontaine said. She turned to their guide. "I cannot thank you enough, sir."

"Aye, don't thank me yet," Cookie said. "And don't be calling me 'sir.' It's just 'Cookie' for you, my lady." He held out his arm, and Fontaine put her fingers on it with a giggle. Rosemary was too nauseated to feel jealous. She craved fresh air with a fierceness that overwhelmed any other sensation. She lurched over to the tiny porthole and stared greedily out until her stomach gave another loud groan.

"I think your companion has had about enough," Cookie said. Then, louder, "You'll want to be followin' me now, my lady."

Silence followed that statement until Rosemary realized Cookie had been speaking to her.

"I'm not... a lady," Rosemary said. Then she belched and nearly cast up her accounts.

Cookie charged across the room and scooped Rosemary into his arms. It was done so quickly and smoothly that she didn't have time to scream or complain. The only sound that escaped her lips was a yelp before Cookie ran out of the room, down the hall, and up several flights of stairs. The next thing Rosemary knew, she was standing on the deck of the ship, clutching a railing, with cool wind brushing through her hair. She closed her eyes and tightened all of her muscles until the sick-sour taste at the back of her throat faded.

"Has it passed?" Fontaine asked.

Rosemary opened her eyes to find the dowager baroness standing beside her with a worried look on her face. Cookie was nowhere in sight, which was a relief, as Rosemary didn't know what the sailor would think if he saw Fontaine rubbing circles in the small of Rosemary's back.

"Here," Fontaine said. She lifted her other hand, holding a chunk of something yellow and bulbous. Ginger root.

"Cookie gave it to me," Fontaine said. "It's apparently an old sailors' remedy."

Rosemary picked up the item and carefully nibbled the end. It had a mild, slightly spicy taste, and a stringy texture, but it was not unpleasant. She bit off a chunk, chewed the ginger in her back teeth, then slipped the rest into her pocket and stared into the far distance. All the while, Fontaine remained beside her, a silent but reassuring presence.

"Have you spoken to the captain yet?" Rosemary asked, when she no longer felt as if the ground were going to open and swallow her up.

Fontaine sighed. "Not yet. I rather hoped he might not find out until we had set sail."

"Too late for that, my lady," a deep voice said.

Rosemary spun around and met the gaze of a man wearing a bright-red suit jacket and trousers. In one hand, he held the top of a cane, and in the other, a rolled-up sheet of paper.

"Thought you could trick me, did you, lass?" the man asked. "Well, I'm not sorry to be telling you that my men inform me of everything that happens on this ship, including Cookie, generously upgrading you and your brood."

"C-Captain Charles, I can explain," Fontaine said. She darted a glance at Rosemary, then continued. "These children—"

"Orphans," the captain said, interrupting. "Orphans who've got nowhere else to go, isn't that, right?"

Fontaine furrowed her brow in a tremendously adorable manner. "Yes, that is right."

The captain nodded. "Then there's nothing else that needs explaining." He lifted his cane and swept it toward them. "Cookie, show these ladies back to their room."

The bald-headed sailor who had helped them before appeared as the captain turned and walked away, leaning heavily on his cane.

Chapter Fourteen

As Fontaine looped her arm with Rosemary's, she felt a sense of impending doom. How was it possible that the captain accepted the intrusion of five children onto his vessel without even demanding payment? It was too much of a coincidence, the latest in a series of strokes of good fortune, that only made her more cautious. When she had lived on the streets, there had been a saying: bad luck strikes true after three. After three incidents of good luck, something awful was certain to happen.

So as Cookie led them back down the stairs, she mentally prepared to be shown to a room that was so horrid that it would make the workhouse seem luxurious in comparison. She could not imagine the captain being so charitable that he would not punish her for tricking him. Still, whatever price she had to pay would be worth it.

Cookie stopped at a door on the same deck as where they had left the children and creaked it open.

"The captain gives his regrets," Cookie said. "This is all that's left for the taking, unless you'll be preferring to sleep on deck with the night crew."

She stepped inside and gulped. The captain's punishment was immediately apparent, although she doubted he understood the implication of his choice. The tiny room contained only one narrow bed bolted to the wall.

Her cheeks heated. There was barely space for two women to *stand* side by side. They wouldn't be able to hide anything from each other. She couldn't ask Rosemary to subject herself to such conditions. No matter how much Fontaine wanted to surrender herself to the heat that simmered between them, she could not. Even if the chance of Mr. Hill discovering what she had done was extremely small, she would not risk losing her spot on the board.

She turned, prepared to tell Cookie that she would sleep with the crew, when Rosemary said, "This will do."

Fontaine gaped. "It will?"

But Cookie was already gone, leaving them alone in the tiny room.

"Are you sure?" Fontaine asked. "I could sleep on the floor with the children. I don't want you to feel…" She couldn't finish that sentence because she wasn't sure what she was feeling herself. One second, she feared Rosemary would demand they find the captain and tell him they could not share a room and the next, she imagined lying beside Rosemary on the thin cot night after night, aching with need. She didn't know which would be worse.

"I'm sure," Rosemary said without looking at her. "We can manage, even if it is hotter than an oven. I don't know what I was thinking, wearing something so heavy." She reached her thumb and forefinger into her hair and tugged out a pin, releasing a thick, curling lock that fell to her waist. Several more locks followed before Fontaine realized she was about to watch her friend undress.

"I-I'll see if our bags have been delivered," Fontaine said. She made a quick retreat, then leaned against the closed door until she caught her breath. Rosemary was striking when she was wrapped up in the many layers of clothing required of a lady. How much more attractive would she be wearing nothing at all?

She imagined a nude Rosemary running her hands down her waist to her hips, a coquettish smile on her face.

Thick, sluggish heat curled in Fontaine's abdomen and made

her itch to reach between her skirts to bring herself relief. Unfortunately, she did not have the leisure to indulge her own desires. There were children only a few doors down who needed her.

She smoothed the wrinkles out of her shirtwaist, then strode down the hall, head held high.

The next two hours were spent answering questions about their destination, breaking up fights over who got each bunk, and making sure Quinn was as comfortable as she could make him. When the room was finally quiet, she checked her timepiece and mentally cursed. It was late. Neither she nor the children had eaten since the morning.

A rap came at the door. Annie and Peter both sat up, eyes wide.

"Who is it?" Annie whispered.

Fontaine shushed her, then padded to the door and creaked it open. Cookie stood outside holding a bulging oil-cloth sack. His shoulders were curved inward, and he wore a nervous expression, like a schoolboy who had been caught doing something naughty. He thrust his bundle toward her. "Cap'n thought the orphans might be hungry."

"Thank you," she said before she was mobbed from behind by children. She snatched the sack out of Cookie's arms before they could take it from him, then made them sit in a circle before she laid their bounty atop the empty cloth in the center of the room. When she was done, their unusual picnic held slices of crusty bread, firm cheese with a heavy rind, cured meat, and a dozen green apples. The children watched her every movement with rapt attention, even Annie, who hardly ever seemed to stop talking.

"Peter, can you divide the food up equally?" Fontaine asked. The young boy seemed to be the most responsible, perhaps because of his dedication to his brother.

Peter straightened his shoulders and beamed. "Of course, my lady."

She groaned. Cookie and the other sailors had taken up referring to her in such a manner, and it seemed it had caught on with the children. The last thing she wanted was to be reminded of her status at every turn, but she did not want to reprimand Peter after everything he had been through. She would smile and bear with the politeness, even if what she really wanted to do was remind them she hadn't always been a lady.

The children were remarkably fair in their distribution of food. There was no complaining or grabbing for more than their share, although Annie and Peter both accepted extras from the younger children who did not finish everything they had been allocated and distributed the excess to Quinn. To her further surprise, all of them calmly returned to their beds when they'd finished eating. All Fontaine had to do was pick up the cloth and brush a few crumbs onto the floor. She wished she had a broom with which to sweep up the mess, but it was not worth disrupting the children further by finding one and returning.

She struggled through the rocking ship back to the single, cramped room she had agreed to share with Rosemary. What had she been thinking? It was difficult enough to keep her hands off her friend without them being pressed together in a narrow cot while the ship rocked them back and forth. They barely had enough room to store their bags without tripping over them.

Her stomach was full of bubbles as she entered the room to find Rosemary sitting on the edge of the bed, stripped down to her shift and stockings.

Fontaine could not stop herself from taking in all of Rosemary, from her slipper-clad feet, up her shapely curves to the swell of her breasts, nipples faintly visible beneath the two layers of thin fabric, to her flushed face, her hair loose down her back. With the moonlight shining through the porthole and making the fabric nearly transparent, she seemed like an angel draped in celestial robes.

Rosemary crossed her arms over her ample bosom and turned her head toward the bed. "Do you wish to have the side by the wall, or the other?"

Another burst of heat rippled out from her core. The bed was even narrower than she had remembered, a scrap of a thing tucked against the wall, hardly more than she had used when she'd been an orphan. And she would sleep next to Rosemary every night for the coming week, or however long it took to reach their destination.

God help her, she would be lucky if she could sleep at all with Rosemary's warm body pressed to hers.

"You can have the wall," Fontaine choked out.

Rosemary jerked her head up and down in a nod, then crawled into the bed so that her back was to Fontaine, giving some manner of privacy. It was a kind gesture, although the view of the curve of Rosemary's waist and rear beneath the thin blanket was just as distracting. She wondered how well their bodies would fit together and then shook her head. They would sleep with their backs to each other. That was the only logical conclusion.

She removed her gown layer by layer, being careful to fold each item before putting it back in her bag. By the end of the trip, she wouldn't own a scrap of unrumpled fabric, but there was little she could do without a lady's maid. There hadn't been time or funds to hire a replacement for Jones. They would have to rely on themselves and let the children take care of each other. It was perhaps a good thing that they were accustomed to doing everything on their own.

When she was down to only her shift, she put her knee on the bed and moved as slowly as she could, positioning her body so that her back was pressed tightly to Rosemary's. That was the best she could do.

Unfortunately, her body refused to give into rest. She felt every inch of Rosemary. Her firm buttocks. The hard ridge of her spine. Her hand moving along Fontaine's hip.

What?

She sucked in a breath. There was most definitely a hand

touching her hip, creeping toward her waist. She wanted that hand to dip between her legs while at the same time her breasts were heavy and longing to be cupped and touched. Every slight movement of Rosemary's hand sent a fresh wave of sensation to her sex until she was certain the dampness she was generating had pooled on the mattress.

There was a shuffle on the bed, then Rosemary was cuddling her with one arm looped over her stomach. The feeling of breasts pressed to her back was so startling that she hovered on the edge of completion without ever touching herself.

But Rosemary did not continue to move her hand, and when Fontaine listened closer, she vaguely heard snoring.

Rosemary was asleep.

She suppressed a groan. She had thought… impossible things. Things that could never be. God, how she had wanted Rosemary to touch her, to make the most of the short time they shared.

She was tempted to reach between her legs and bring herself the relief she craved, but that might cause Rosemary to wake, and she didn't want the other woman to be repulsed. Kissing was one thing, but bringing sexual pleasure to each other was far different. She would not ask Rosemary to do anything with which she was not comfortable.

So, even though it was very difficult to fall asleep while knowing whom she was clasped against, Fontaine closed her eyes and slowly, ever so slowly, let the warmth of Rosemary's body lull her into a fitful sleep.

Chapter Fifteen

T HE NEXT MORNING, Rosemary strolled through the narrow corridors of the ship, chewing a chunk of ginger with her back teeth and bracing herself against the wall with one hand. The constant swaying continued to upset her stomach, although none of the children had been similarly affected. Annie scampered past her, bare feet squeaking on the wooden plank floor as if she had been seafaring for years instead of barely more than a day.

She had expected most of her time during the journey to be spent keeping the orphans out of the way of the guests, but the children were more interested in the sailors. This might have been a problem, except that the sailors, unaccustomed to having children aboard, delighted in their antics and questions. She hoped that would be the case for many days so that they would not have to entertain them.

"Wait for us!" Peter cried from behind her, and then both he and a pale Quinn stumbled past her. Quinn's fever had broken, although his breathing was still raspy. The movement of his passing caused the flounced ruffles on the neckline of her bodice to flutter and made her reconsider her choice of outfit. She had done without a crinoline, but the hem of her cream, linen walking suit was already stained a dingy brown from being dragged across the ground.

She should have returned to the small cabin, but she didn't want to risk seeing Fontaine and remembering what they'd nearly done. Even if Fontaine's skin had been silky soft beneath her fingers, and the way she had responded to Rosemary's touch had awakened something deep inside her.

A shiver rippled up her back. They had many nights before they arrived in Halifax. How could she possibly resist sharing pleasure with Fontaine when they were pressed together in the tiny bed every night? Especially when they had a door with a lock. There was no reason anyone ever needed to know what they had done. They could indulge themselves fully with the confidence they would not be discovered.

The ship gave another lurch, causing her to stumble forward and nearly choke on her ginger. She swallowed the chunk, and her stomach gurgled in displeasure.

Basil had died on a ship. She often wondered what his last thoughts had been before the icy water had swallowed him up. Had he agonized over the decisions that had led him to that moment or had he accepted death with peace?

Air. She needed fresh air.

She reached the end of the hall and a set of stairs that seemed to go up forever. By the time she'd reached the top, she was sweating with exertion, but the cool wind that whirled around her immediately made the trip worthwhile. She rushed over to the spot Cookie had taken her the previous day and grasped the railing with both hands, squinting against the harsh rays of the sun. After a few minutes, the gurgling in her stomach calmed, and she forcibly relaxed her stiff arms and shoulders. Despite the unpleasantness of her seasickness, she had to admit the view was stunning. The sky was painted in shades of red and orange above the frothing, dark-blue waves of the ocean. Large, white birds skimmed the surface of the water in the distance, and the sails flapped rhythmically above her.

She released a long breath and turned, intending to return to the warmer interior of the boat, only for her gaze to be drawn to two figures sitting on stools near the towering mast.

The first was Cookie, the muscular, tattooed man who had

helped them board. The second was Winter.

"Shouldn't you be with the others, Winter?" she asked softly as she came to stand beside the pair.

Winter dipped his head.

"Don't mind," Cookie said. "Nice to have someone to talk to. Look at this, Winter. Watch my hands."

The sailor twined three strands of rope, forming a braid. She was certain he could have done the task much faster, but he moved with deliberate slowness.

"Copy me, Winter," he said.

Winter shot a glance at her before reaching into the bucket and retrieving three lengths of rope. He watched Cookie do several more loops before hesitantly copying the movements.

She clasped her forearms in her hands, unsure if Cookie was merely being kind, or if he had a genuine interest in taking the child on as an apprentice. If the former, she should gently remind Winter not to occupy too much of the sailor's time.

If the latter…

"What's this?" Fontaine asked, appearing so suddenly that Winter startled and dropped his rope.

The hair on Rosemary's arms rose as she faced the dowager baroness. The events of the previous night seemed to hang in the air between them, a kind of electricity that made it difficult to meet the other woman's gaze. She was acutely aware of how Fontaine's curves filled out her dress, rumpled as it was. Nor could she forget what Fontaine's rear had felt like, pressed to her front, or the soft sounds she'd made in her sleep.

Her cheeks heated as she realized she was staring. She cleared her throat and gestured to the sailor and orphan. "Winter has been keeping Cookie company."

Cookie grunted, his gaze never leaving the rope in his hands. He had increased the speed of his movements. Winter furrowed his brow as he attempted to keep up.

"Winter, don't you want to go and play?" Fontaine asked.

The boy shook his head without stopping his task. His small fingers made quick work of the braid, and he was rapidly approaching the same speed as the sailor, although his loops were not nearly as tight or even as Cookie's.

Winter finished his work, placed it aside, then clasped his hands in his lap and stared at Cookie with rapt attention. A few seconds later, Cookie put down his own braid and picked up Winter's, easing his fingers over the loops. When he finished, he grunted and set the braid aside. "It'll do."

Winter grinned and reached into the bucket for another set of strands.

Rosemary guided Fontaine away from the pair. "Those two are getting along well."

Fontaine bit her lip and furrowed her brow. A remarkable distraction. Rosemary wished she could press her own lips to Fontaine's, smooth away the wrinkles on her forehead with her fingers.

"Perhaps Captain Charles might be interested in taking Winter on as an apprentice," Fontaine said. "He is a respectable man. He would take good care of Winter..." She sighed. "But the apprentice premium. We don't have the funds. Even Captain Charles is unlikely to take on the responsibility of another mouth to feed when a child cannot provide the same labor as an adult." She touched the gold sparkling in her ears.

"No," Rosemary said. She knew exactly what Fontaine was thinking. The daft woman was about to give up her jewels for a child she had only met a few days prior. "You don't have to do this. We could find another way."

Fontaine glanced at Cookie and Winter across the deck, and a softness came over her expression. At that moment, it was obvious that she had decided, and it would be pointless to argue with her. Rosemary wished she could make it easier on Fontaine, but it was her choice to do what she wished with her possessions, even if Rosemary felt that by the time the journey ended, Fontaine would have barely a shilling to her person.

Then again, hadn't Rosemary done the same thing for Saffron, Angelica, and Basil? With the baronet's fortune nearly depleted, she'd spent her meager widow's portion, sold her jewels, hired a governess, all so the children would have everything they needed. She knew exactly how it felt to feel responsible for another person, even if that person was not directly related by blood.

"Fine. Let's speak to the captain."

ROSEMARY WASN'T SURE what she'd expected to find in a captain's quarters, but the space they stood in was as cluttered as it was luxurious. A thick, red-and-gold rug lay on the floor, the walls were covered with pegs holding mysterious, bronze objects, and a single large table dominated the room, a map spread across its surface.

"I thought you might consider taking Winter on as an apprentice," Fontaine said.

Captain Charles's eyebrows rose all the way to his hairline. "I have noticed Cookie taking an interest in the boy."

"He'll be as hard-working as any other man on your crew," Fontaine said quickly. "Street children are accustomed to making their own way."

The captain put his folded hands on top of the map. "How do you propose to pay the apprentice's price?"

"I will pay it," Rosemary said, at the same time that Fontaine said, "My earrings."

Rosemary jerked her head toward the dowager baroness. "No."

Fontaine had been wearing those earrings since the day they'd met. Obviously, they meant a great deal to her. Rosemary leaned in to whisper in her ear. "I have the funds."

She had packed a small amount of money that Saffron had gifted her a few weeks before.

Fontaine tilted her head and lowered her eyelids but did not meet Rosemary's gaze. "These children are my responsibility, not yours."

The words burrowed into Rosemary's skin and plunged into her heart. After all the effort she'd put into rescuing Winter and the others, Fontaine wouldn't let her help. Perhaps she'd seen what Rosemary had already realized, that she would never be the kind of person who could naturally empathize with others the way Fontaine could. The best she could muster was a kind of cold sympathy that bordered on pity. No wonder Basil had fled her house. She'd piled expectations and responsibilities upon him without sparing a second to consider how he'd felt.

She stepped back. "Fine."

Fontaine faced the captain and lifted her trembling fingers to her ears. "My earrings. They're diamond and gold. They…They belonged to my mother."

Captain Charles tapped his fingers on the top of his desk. "You'd be willing to part with such valuable, sentimental items for a child you barely know?"

Fontaine straightened her back. "It is my duty to see the orphans settled in appropriate positions."

Captain Charles rubbed his chin again. "I am reluctant to agree to allow a child to remain on this ship, but perhaps it is what we need. Some young blood." He nodded. "I agree." Then he held out his hand.

Fontaine removed her earrings and dropped them into Captain Charles's palm. He closed his fingers. "The boy can move into Cookie's room tomorrow. He'll board with him for as long as his apprenticeship lasts."

"Oh." Fontaine blinked. "I suppose, then…" She looked at Rosemary. "We won't have to share after tonight. I could take Winter's bed with the children."

It should have been a relief. She would have privacy, and a bed to herself. There would be no more close encounters where temptation overwhelmed her logic. She would accept the situation and be grateful for it.

Even if she longed for Fontaine at night.

Chapter Sixteen

T HE REST OF the day passed in a dreary haze. Rosemary kept her distance from Fontaine, unable to find the right words to express her frustration that they would have only one more night together. She walked laps of the third-class decks for hours, considering and rejecting ways to ask Fontaine if she wanted to do more than sleep. But when she eventually arrived at their room, her pulse skittering beneath her skin, it was to find the lights extinguished and Fontaine undressed and lying with her back to the door.

Fighting back a surge of disappointment, Rosemary hastily removed her many layers before slipping into the bed. She stayed as far away from the other woman as she could, but the tight confines meant she could still feel the warmth of Fontaine's body and hear her soft exhales. It was a particular torture that made her briefly consider the option of sleeping with the night crew.

Then Fontaine curved around her from behind and tucked her arm around Rosemary's stomach. The sudden warmth made her want to roll over and find Fontaine's lips, but she couldn't be sure if the other woman was awake and teasing her, or merely a restless sleeper.

She closed her eyes and imagined Fontaine cupping her breasts, squeezing and kneading her flesh. One hand would slide down her stomach and, without lifting the fabric, press Rosemary's nether lips apart…

She was so wet, and panting from the imagined scenario, that she hardly recognized Fontaine's tongue on her neck. It wasn't until the dowager baroness tweaked her nipple that Rosemary yelped and nearly leaped from the bed. Only the arm around her chest kept her in place.

"I was dreaming about you," Fontaine said.

Rosemary gulped. "What kind of dream?"

"A most pleasant one."

Rosemary exhaled a long breath as Fontaine's hand gently cupped her breast. There was only a thin layer of cambric lying between Fontaine's fingers and her nipple. The warmth curling in her belly throbbed. She wanted Fontaine's fingers tucked between her legs, rubbing circles and delving deep inside her. Her own hands itched with the need to touch. To feel Fontaine spasming around her fingers. To lick the traces of pleasure that dripped down her legs.

She remembered the first time she'd tasted a woman's sex. It had been far more pleasurable than putting her mouth on her husband's cock. The soft folds of a woman's vulva didn't throb or grow large inside her mouth. A woman would never, even unintentionally, choke her partner by thrusting her sexual organs down their throat.

One of Fontaine's legs shifted over Rosemary's hips and pulled her even tighter back. Then, to Rosemary's immense pleasure, Fontaine drifted one of her hands lower.

Lower…

"Please," Rosemary whispered.

Fontaine continued, rubbing every inch of her skin in a casual massage before finally reaching her navel. Those questing, curious fingers tickled her stomach, then brushed the edge of the crinkly hair at the apex of her thighs before sliding even lower.

So close…

Any moment, she would wake up, and she would be back to a quivering bundle of need. She could not achieve orgasm in her sleep, of that she was certain. But God, she wanted the dream to go on forever.

Fontaine twirled the tip of her finger in just such a way that Rosemary gasped and moved her hips into the motion. It felt so *good*. Electric sensations shot down her legs, and the pressure in her pelvis built to a crescendo.

She flipped around so she was facing Fontaine and pressed their mouths together. The sounds that came from Fontaine's throat were almost enough to push her over the edge.

"More?" Fontaine whispered.

"Oh, yes," Rosemary said. "Much more."

Fontaine plunged her fingers deep and pleasure washed over Rosemary in a wave. When it receded, she brought her hands up to cup the heavy mounds of Fontaine's breasts.

"My turn."

Fontaine pulled off her shift, then grabbed the edge of Rosemary's and lifted it over her head. With their naked bodies twined together, Rosemary touched her mouth to Fontaine's nipple and rasped, then suckled deeply. Fontaine bucked beneath her, but Rosemary held her down with one hand on her hip. Then she slid her palm down until her fingers brushed the wiry hair covering Fontaine's vulva. She lifted her lips and blew gently on the now-wet nipple, making Fontaine shudder before turning her attention to the other nipple, while gently pressing her fingers against Fontaine's vulva without quite reaching inside. When she had properly sucked on both of Fontaine's nipples and tasted every inch of skin above her navel, she scooted down the bed and spread Fontaine's legs apart, revealing every luxurious inch of her.

"You look delicious," she whispered. "Can I taste you?"

Fontaine gave a throaty laugh. "Please do."

Rosemary slid her fingers inside Fontaine's vulva, between the outer and inner lips in a V. The folds of her vulva were different, but also the same. Her inner lips were longer, the hair covering her *mons pubis* thicker, and her clitoris larger. Rosemary devoured the sight. She might not have another chance to enjoy herself.

A bead of liquid slid down from Fontaine's entrance and absorbed into the mattress.

That would not do.

She licked in one solid rasp from her entrance to her clitoris. Fontaine moaned and pressed her hips upward. Rosemary pushed her down, sliding her tongue into Fontaine's vulva, savoring every layer before moving on to the next. By the time she had reached the innermost layers, Fontaine was panting and squirming beneath her.

Compared to her former partners, Fontaine was all sweet curves. Even the gentle musk coming from her body was sweeter. Her taste was mildly salty, but not unpleasant.

She slid her finger around Fontaine's entrance, then slowly pressed until two knuckles were inside. When she found the right spot, she crooked her fingers, causing Fontaine to gasp and whimper. She wrapped her lips around Fontaine's clitoris and sucked, then added a second finger and continued her scooping movement. The quivering of Fontaine's flesh told her that her climax was coming. When it did, she plunged deep, savoring each moment of shuddering release.

The moment seemed to last forever, but eventually, Fontaine stilled.

Rosemary crawled back up and cuddled her from behind. Her hair was slick with sweat, and she didn't know when she would have a chance to bathe. Fresh water for bathing seemed as if it would be a rarity aboard a ship. But she would spend a month without bathing if it meant she got to spend every morning with Fontaine in her arms.

"I wish every morning could be like this," Fontaine said, echoing Rosemary's thoughts.

Rosemary stilled. She had intentionally avoided considering what would happen when they arrived in Halifax. They were safe from scandal while she acted as Fontaine's companion, but not knowing what awaited them made Rosemary nervous. Despite doing her best to keep distant, she had grown accustomed to the orphans. She would dearly miss Annie's energetic singing and the gentle way Peter doted on Quinn. For the first time in longer than she could remember, she wondered if she had made a mistake by not remarrying and having children of her own. But her nieces and nephew *had* been her children, no matter what anyone else said.

The sound of rapidly approaching footfalls and high-pitched laughter jolted her out of her thoughts. She rolled off the bed and struggled into her garments, sliding them over her sweat-slick skin. She kept her back to the dowager baroness, certain any words that came to her would muddle together if she tried to speak. A casual sexual encounter aboard the ship was one thing, but she was only torturing herself by imagining anything more.

Fontaine had commitments. Responsibilities. She had to maintain a reputation in society. The orphans of London depended on her charity. Any future they shared would require secrecy and lies.

"Where are you going?" Fontaine asked.

Rosemary swallowed the knot in her throat. As painful as it was, she knew what she had to do.

"Rosemary?" Fontaine whispered.

She had to be strong. If Fontaine didn't have the strength to stay away, then it was up to her.

"I think I heard Annie just now," she said without turning. "I'll go check and make sure everyone is in bed."

She reached for the doorknob but couldn't quite make herself turn it.

"Are you coming back?" Fontaine asked.

Rosemary shuddered as she opened the door. "I think we both know it's better if I don't."

Chapter Seventeen

O N THE EIGHTH day of their journey, when Rosemary was nauseated merely looking at the soiled clothes she would have to wear once again, she met a guest transporting textile goods and bartered one of the three dresses she had packed for several yards of soft-gray cotton and a sewing kit. She took her bounty to her cabin and formed a rough skirt, which she paired with a silver suit jacket. As she strolled down the hall toward the crew mess hall in search of luncheon, her drab reflection flitted past each porthole like a ghost.

Every member of their group, aside from her, seemed to have settled into routines. The children slept until late morning, ate a small breakfast in the crew mess hall, then returned to their room, where they learned what to expect when they arrived in Halifax from Fontaine. Rosemary had attempted to join these sessions, only to find that she was more of a hindrance than a help. Rather than pay attention, the children would poke at her dress or whisper naughty things they had overheard from sailors into her ear. Quinn was the most mischievous; having recovered most remarkably, the boy was now a bundle of energy.

So she spent most of her time wandering the second- and third-class decks each afternoon as Fontaine joined the other guests of the *ton* in the grand saloon and the children found small jobs to do, mending sails or assisting in the kitchen. Even Winter took to his new role with gusto. He boasted about his apprenticeship to everyone who was willing to listen about the calluses forming on his palms and followed Cookie around like a duckling.

"Pardon me, madam."

She spun around to find a man standing behind her. He was several inches shorter than her and wore a black suit that clung to his thin frame. Like all the other gentlemen aboard, he wore his facial hair such that there was no distinction between where his hair ended and his mustache began, although his chin was clean shaven.

"Yes?" she asked before noticing the walls behind the man were not drab white but papered in a green, floral pattern. In her aimless strolling, she had ventured onto the first-class deck.

The man gave a deep bow. "Good evening, madam. Forgive my rudeness in not seeking a proper introduction, but I am John Prue."

Rude, indeed, approaching her without first asking someone to introduce them.

"Rosemary Summersby," she said, feeling compelled to give her name, even as Mr. Prue's intense stare made her itch to back away.

"Ah!" The man straightened and beamed. "Excellent. I was hoping to speak to you. Captain Charles told me you are the companion of the Dowager Lady Kerry?"

Rosemary pressed her hands to her waist. "That is correct."

Her gaze was drawn to the guests milling behind him. Each lady and gentleman wore elaborate evening attire. It was easy to imagine Fontaine in that crowd, charming the other guests with her dry wit, gathering sponsors to fund her charitable efforts. It would have been a much more efficient use of her time compared to chaperoning orphans across the ocean. There might even be a place for Rosemary by her side if she continued in her role as companion. If they kept their personal affections limited to private settings, no one would ever have to know they were anything more than friends.

Mr. Prue tugged at the bottom of his suit jacket. "I apologize for my impertinence, Miss Summersby—"

"Mrs.," Rosemary felt compelled to correct.

His smile was pinched. "Mrs. Summersby. But I must speak with Lady Kerry. Do you know where I might find her?"

"I will pass along your request," Rosemary said. She was not about to make it easier for this strange man to find Fontaine without speaking to her first.

"My gratitude," he said. "Well, ah, perhaps you could also extend an invitation to Lady Kerry. I would be pleased to host you both in my suite for luncheon tomorrow."

"I am certain Lady Kerry would be pleased," she said, even as her gaze drifted over his shoulder once again. A stunning woman resplendent in gold silk glanced her way. A moment later, she flicked open her lacy fan and leaned toward the lady standing beside her, who giggled.

Rosemary clutched the fabric of her homespun skirt. After spending the past few days in the company of children and sailors, she had forgotten how quick society was to leap to judgment. She was posing as Fontaine's companion. That meant her actions, her appearance, reflected on the dowager baroness.

Then she caught sight of someone else, and in that moment, her blood ran cold. A familiar man stood in the middle of the line, scowling fiercely.

Mr. Blake, wearing a silver-and-black striped suit.

She blinked, and he was gone. She looked around, certain Mr. Blake had only stepped into the shadows or behind another passenger, but there was no sign of him.

"Is something the matter, Mrs. Summersby?" Mr. Prue asked.

"Please excuse me," she said. Then she spun and quickly retreated down the hall, not stopping until the carpet beneath her feet turned back into wooden planks and the wallpaper vanished from the walls. She had to tell Fontaine that Mr. Blake was on the ship, that he might have been in the carriage they had spotted when they'd been boarding.

Why?

She stumbled to a halt. As far as she knew, there was nothing special about the orphans. To Mr. Blake and whatever unscrupulous individual he was representing as a solicitor, they were likely indistinguishable from any other group of urchins. There was no reason to pursue them when they could simply find replacements.

She turned to a porthole and stared out into the frothy waves. In the moments before spotting Mr. Blake, she'd been preoccupied with what the future would hold. Didn't it make more sense that she had only imagined Mr. Blake, that her mind was trying to invent a reason for her to stay by Fontaine's side? As long as the children were in danger, she could focus on the present, instead of imagining a life with Fontaine beyond their current mission.

She leaned her forehead against the cool glass. She wouldn't tell Fontaine about Mr. Blake. There was no proof, beyond a momentary glimpse, that he was aboard the ship, and Fontaine had enough to worry about.

Rosemary had allowed herself to grow complacent, thinking that they were hundreds of miles away from London and could therefore behave however they wished. But it didn't matter how private their situation seemed—there was always a chance of discovery. She had learned that the hard way when Lady Jarvis had nearly walked in on her kissing an opera singer in Lady Hartwood's library last summer. All it would take was a poorly timed kiss, an overheard whisper of endearment, or an embrace that went on for too long, and the newspapers would be full of stories. Any of the guests could bring whispers back to the *ton*. It was safer to keep her distance from the dowager baroness. Then no one could accuse them of anything inappropriate.

She used her handkerchief to wipe the sweat from her face, then continued down the hall. But when she arrived at her cabin, the door was open and Fontaine stood inside, frowning and twisting the fabric of her lilac, linen skirt in her hands.

"What's wrong?" Rosemary asked. She stepped inside and

closed the door behind her before realizing how terrible of an idea that was. Mere moments after resolving to stay away, they were alone together.

"Oh!" Fontaine dropped her skirt. "I was just..." She bit her lip. "I...I feel as if you have been avoiding me."

Rosemary should have felt something at Fontaine's words, but her interaction with Mr. Prue had left her strangely numb. "I have."

Fontaine blinked several times before dropping her gaze. "I see."

"The risk is too great," Rosemary said, feeling compelled to explain, even though they both understood.

Fontaine nodded. "I know. You are right, of course, but..." She heaved a sigh. "I miss you."

Warmth curled in Rosemary's stomach, chasing away the numbness. "I miss you, too."

Risk be damned.

She stepped forward and wrapped her arms around Fontaine. It felt so right. Like they could do anything together.

Fontaine's shoulders shuddered, and the soft sound of sniffling sent a throb of pain through Rosemary's heart. She drifted her hand lower, rubbing slow circles on Fontaine's back.

"Are you sure you want this?" Fontaine asked.

"I want you so much, it scares me," Rosemary said honestly.

She lifted her hands to Fontaine's chest, rubbing her fingers over the spot where she knew Fontaine's nipples were likely erect and throbbing, as Rosemary's were. She unbuttoned the front of Fontaine's blouse and touched the bare skin of her shoulders. To her pleasure, Fontaine had done without a corset. The faint shapes of her nipples were visible beneath the sheer layer of her shift.

"Yes," Fontaine whispered, throwing her neck back. "Touch me."

Rosemary removed her gloves, then fluttered her fingers over Fontaine's breasts, making her gasp.

"More?" Rosemary whispered. Part of her wanted Fontaine to say *no*, wanted her to pull away and cover her chest with her arms. Then she would have a firm answer, and the blurred boundaries between them would solidify into walls.

But instead of rejection, Fontaine wrapped her arms about Rosemary's neck and brought their mouths together in a searing kiss. Rosemary clasped Fontaine's hips, anchoring her in place. The dowager baroness tasted like ale, slightly bitter and fruity.

She was about to draw Fontaine down to the mattress when a rap came at the door. She dropped her hands and stumbled back, then hurriedly wiped her mouth with the back of her hand.

"Mrs. Summersby, are you there?"

"The captain," Fontaine whispered.

"One moment," Rosemary exclaimed.

Fontaine hurriedly put her clothing back in order and hid behind the door, which was silly because no one would question them being in the same room together after they had already spent two nights sharing a bed. Rosemary's lips curved as she opened the door to obscure Fontaine from Captain Charles, who stood with his hat in his hands.

"Pardon the intrusion," he said. "I thought I should inform you we will be arriving in Halifax tomorrow."

As she thanked the captain and closed the door, Fontaine shimmied out of her hiding spot and adjusted her bodice, her lips pressed into a thin line.

"I'll tell the children," she said, flicking a stray curl out of her face. "I'll come find you after."

The huskiness in her voice made Rosemary gulp. The coldness that had settled between them over the past few days seemed to have melted. It was enough to make her hope that whatever lodging they procured next had a sturdy bed. But as Fontaine squeezed around the door, bringing their hips into close contact, Rosemary remembered what had happened before she'd arrived at her room.

"I met a man this afternoon," she said. "He asked me to relay an invitation to afternoon lunch to you. Mr. John Prue."

"I have no interest in entertaining *men*," Fontaine said. Then she pressed a quick kiss to Rosemary's lips before striding down the hall. Rosemary's gaze remained on Fontaine's hips until she vanished around a corner. Then Rosemary removed a handkerchief from her pocket and dabbed the sweat from her suddenly warm face.

Chapter Eighteen

ROSEMARY STOOD AT the back of the line of children, holding her valise in one hand and waving to Cookie and Winter with the other. Unlike the previous day, the sky today was slate gray, and a slight drizzle had dampened every surface and scrap of fabric. Halifax spread out before them, squat buildings dotting the land as far as she could see.

She chose her steps carefully as she followed Annie down the gangplank and onto the bustling dock. Cookie had piled their bags next to the main road, where Fontaine was speaking to a man in a black slicker coat, presumably arranging transportation. The clang of bells, shouting of merchants, and roar of waves hitting the shore made it impossible to hear anything Fontaine said, even though she was only a few feet away.

Annie curled her fingers into Rosemary's hand.

"What is it?" Rosemary asked, leaning over so she could hear Annie's response over the cacophony.

"It stinks," Annie said.

She was not wrong. The rank smell of sewage combined with the fishy aroma of the nearby market tangled in her nostrils and made her nauseated. It was a painful reminder of London and the family she had left behind. She hoped the letters she'd sent Saffron and Angelica before she'd left would keep them from worrying too much. The moment they were settled, she would write again and assure her nieces that she was well.

"Ugh," Annie said. She wrinkled her nose and lifted her sleeve to her face.

Rosemary removed a perfumed handkerchief from her pocket and handed it to Annie, who draped it over her face.

"—robbery!" Fontaine cried.

Rosemary straightened and pushed through the children to stand by the baroness, whose cheeks were bright red.

"What's wrong?" Rosemary asked.

Fontaine gestured to the man sitting in the driver's seat of the enormous coach in front of them. "Five pounds! That's what he's demanding to bring us to the Halifax office. It's—It's—" She crossed her arms and scowled. "That is robbery, sir."

The man shrugged and flicked his reins. The two black horses attached to his conveyance plodded away, leaving them standing next to their bags with no way of getting to their destination.

"What now?" Rosemary asked. Several of the sailors milling around them drew closer, casting appraising glances at their belongings. The children closed ranks the way they had in the workhouse, with Annie and Peter standing between the younger ones and the adults.

Fontaine put her hands in her hair and groaned. "I don't know. I'm sorry. I—"

"The lady did right," an unfamiliar voice said.

As Rosemary peered through the crowd for the speaker, there was a chirruping sound. A mud-splattered cab led by two mottled, gray horses appeared and took the place of the departed coach. The driver wore a black overcoat that was crisscrossed with seams, as if someone had ripped the garment into pieces and then sewn it back together. He slipped down from his post and removed his bowler hat, revealing a face as heavily lined as his coat.

"'Tis a scam they've got goin'." He spoke with a peculiar accent where the vowels were softened, and the ends of words were left off. "Offerin' a ride to new arrivals who don't know the currency." He nodded to Fontaine. "You did right. Proper fare's a dollar per person."

"A 'dollar,'" Rosemary repeated. Out of the corner of her eye, she watched Xavier place his hand on the flank of one of the cab's horses.

"The local currency," Fontaine said. She reached into her pocket, removed several silver coins, and handed them to the man. "Captain Charles traded some of his dollars for my pounds this morning. Will this suffice, ah…sir?"

"James," he said. Then he flicked his hand, and the coins vanished. "Aye, it'll do. Where will I be takin' you lot?"

"1416 Arcadia Avenue," Fontaine said.

James leaned back on his heels and clicked his tongue. "Quite sure o' that? Nothin' but a mess down Arcadia."

The disapproval in his voice reminded Rosemary of the way Mr. Blake had spoken when he'd intruded on the meeting in the salon. Like a man who didn't believe a woman could do anything of value on her own.

"Yes," Fontaine said, crisply. "The Halifax Home for Destitute Children is our destination."

James shrugged. "Arcadia it is. Now get the children inside, 'afore the locals take more interest. You, too, boy. Bertha ain't got much patience."

Xavier flinched away from the horse he had been patting.

Several men who had been staring at them shifted. Gooseflesh erupted on Rosemary's arms.

"It's time to go, everyone," Fontaine said as she opened the door to the cab.

Thankfully, the children did not need to be told twice and scampered inside.

James loaded the bags atop the cab quickly, suggesting to Rosemary that she was not the only one who felt tension winding around her. Every time she turned her head, someone was gazing at them. Then they were off, and Rosemary felt as if every bone in her body vibrated as they maneuvered through the crowded market.

"Why can't we stay with you?" Annie asked. "I don't want to go to another workhouse."

Fontaine winced. "It's not a workhouse. It's, ah, well, it's not an orphanage, either. It's…a good place."

"How can you be sure?" Peter asked, clutching his brother's hand. Both boys wore the same fearful expression as they had the day Rosemary and Fontaine had rescued them from the workhouse. That fear tugged at something in Rosemary's heart and made her reach out and touch the boy's shoulders.

"We won't leave until we're certain it's a good place. A safe place."

The boys glanced at each other and relaxed fractionally, but the atmosphere in the cab remained tense as they crossed a bridge and ventured away from the city center. Towering, nondescript buildings made way for sprawling homes with bright-green lawns, which then transformed into battered structures that jut out of the ground like jagged teeth, surrounded by wide swaths of empty land. The farther they drove, taking one branching street after another, the more she felt as if something were wrong. Why would a charitable organization that specialized in taking in children from across the ocean place their office so far from the docks?

She glanced across the cab, prepared to ask Fontaine if she was certain they were headed in the right direction, when the cab slowed to a stop, and she heard the shushing sound of James sliding off his post.

She peered out the window, searching for any sign that might indicate they had arrived at their destination, but the few buildings near them were half-complete, vacated, as if the construction crews assigned to them had vanished before finishing their tasks.

"Wait here, children," Fontaine said. She maneuvered to the door and opened it to reveal the scorched ruins of a house.

Rosemary stepped over Peter and Quinn to exit the cab, closing the door behind her.

"What is this?" Fontaine asked James, her voice pitched high. "I told you to bring us to 1416 Arcadia Avenue."

"Aye, you did," he said. "It burnt down three weeks past. I thought you were knowing this and wanted to see the mess for yourself."

Rosemary crossed the street to the ruins. Blackened, wooden beams stuck out of the ground like the ribcage of a giant. The few remaining windows held shattered panes of glass, and tattered curtains waved in the wind.

She approached a fallen square of wood, in much better condition than anything else around it. She picked it up and used a handkerchief to rub the dirty surface. The words written on the plank were nearly illegible, but she could make out the final two: *Destitute Children.*

It was the home they had come to visit.

She brought the sign to Fontaine, who gasped when she looked at it.

"It can't be," she said. Then her knees buckled, and Rosemary barely had time to drop the sign and wrap an arm around the dowager baroness before she crumpled to the ground.

"No, no, no," Fontaine wailed.

The door to the carriage opened, and the children peered out, unusually silent, their eyes wide.

"How much money do you have with you?" Rosemary asked Fontaine. "I think we might be here for a while."

Chapter Nineteen

"Is THERE NOT a single room available?" Fontaine asked, trying not to let her desperation show.

The owner of the boarding house, a woman wearing a thick application of makeup that didn't quite disguise deep grooves in her skin, pursed her thin lips and crossed her arms over her flour-splattered apron. "I've got nothing on such short notice. You'll have to find somewhere else."

Fontaine clenched her jaw. There *was* nowhere else. They had spent the entire morning searching Halifax for a place to stay, but several hotels had recently been damaged by fires and those that remained were full. The newspapers had reported that only a few bodies had been recovered from the Halifax Home, and only adults. The operator, Mr. Sellinger, was nowhere to be found. She already owed James a hefty sum. The cab driver had ferried them around for hours without complaint.

Perhaps it was her shabby clothing—she hadn't the time to wash her nicer garments before leaving the ship—or the children who were causing proprietors to turn them away. Her reputation in London meant nothing in Halifax, and there were few business owners willing to take pounds instead of the few dollars she possessed.

"Please, Mrs. Wexford," Fontaine said. "I will visit a currency exchanger in the morning. I'll pay any price." When Mrs. Wexford straightened, she added, "Any *reasonable* price."

The woman removed a pack of cigarettes from her pocket, tapped one out, and touched it to her lips. "I suppose there might be something. Last year we did up the attic, intending to host a few *home children*." She curled her lip when she said the last two words.

"'Home children'?" Fontaine repeated.

"You know, the children who were brought over from England." Mrs. Wexford reached into her other pocket, frowned, then patted her sides. "Now where did I..."

Fontaine realized what the woman was looking for and reached into her pocket for her box of matches. She removed the box and held it out in what felt like the first move in a fresh round of bartering. If it encouraged Mrs. Wexford to think more favorably of her, Fontaine would overlook the woman's vices and the callous way she spoke of the children her foundation had shipped to Halifax.

"The attic?" Fontaine asked.

Mrs. Wexford murmured her thanks, lit her cigarette, then took a long draw, leaving a smear of lipstick behind on the white paper. "Three days. Ten dollars. You'd be wise to take it." She exhaled smoke out of her nose. "Street children don't last long here."

Fontaine paused in the action of removing a stack of bills from her pocket. "What do you mean?"

"Snatchers," Mrs. Wexford said. She took another puff. "That's what they're called. They snatch children off the street and take them away."

A wave of cold washed over Fontaine. "Take them where?"

"The country." Mrs. Wexford leaned against the doorframe and held out her hand that was not holding the cigarette, palm up.

Fontaine itched to ask more questions, but she could tell from the woman's tone that she would not answer them. Instead, Fontaine laid several precious bills into the woman's hand, one by one. In the morning, she would have to find someone to exchange the rest of her pounds for dollars. She could not leave until she learned what had happened to the Halifax office and, more importantly, the hundreds of children who had been shipped from London.

Mrs. Wexford gave her the key to the attic, which was accessible from outside by a wooden staircase that wound around the back of the house. Fontaine then returned to James and informed him they had found a place to stay.

"'Tis a blessing," James said. He leaned in his seat atop the coach and tipped his felt hat back. "You be keeping those children off the street past nightfall, madam. Ain't nothin' but snatchers in the dark 'round these parts."

Fontaine put her hands on her hips. "Does the entire city know about these 'snatchers'?"

James shrugged and slid down from his post. "Most know someone who's been snatched." He put a hand on the flank of one of his horses. The mottled beast stamped its rear leg and snorted, releasing a cloud of mist. "Used to have a 'prentice. Two weeks back, sent the boy to the cobbler near twilight." His throat worked. "Ain't seen him since. That's what the snatchers do."

The way he spoke those words, so casually, as if it happened every day, sent another shiver down Fontaine's back. "Do you know where they're taking them? Mrs. Wexford would only say 'the country.'"

"If'n, I knew, I would've gone to retrieve my 'prentice already." He grimaced. "If'n, I had to guess, there'd be a lot of them in the gold mines."

An uncomfortable knot formed in Fontaine's stomach. The scenario sounded remarkably similar to what was happening in London. "Are there no laws to prevent such things?"

The moment she'd said the words, she wanted to laugh at her own folly. Her own country had attempted several times to put an end to children working in dangerous conditions, but each bill passed was as ineffectual as the last. Without severe penalties for employers, the enormous value of the labor of children meant the police were as likely to look the other way as to intervene when a case was brought to their attention.

"Laws are only as good as the men set to enforce them," James said, as if reading her mind. "A coin slipped in the right pocket, and when the inspector shows up, there are no children about." He scowled. "They make 'em drive horses. Pull cars. Crawl inside those big, steel machines. The dead 'uns get tossed over the cliffs. No body, no investigation."

Fontaine swallowed hard, even though it felt as if a hand had closed around her throat. How many children had the foundation shipped to Halifax, only for them to live a hard few weeks or months before being cast unceremoniously onto the rocky shore?

James patted his horse's flank again and said, loudly, "You're testing my patience, boy."

"What are you—" Fontaine started, before Xavier scurried out from beneath a horse and ran off.

She had a brief, mental flash of the boy being bundled into an unmarked cab and was about to call his name, when she recognized Rosemary sitting on a bench near a fountain. The boy was joining the rest of the group. Her shoulders sagged. With the momentary surge of fear had come a realization. She couldn't leave the children in Halifax, not when they might be scooped up by the same unknown group that James and Mrs. Wexford had mentioned.

She tried to move, but her body refused. Halifax was supposed to have meant a better life for London's orphans. Not more of the same. During her previous visits to the city, Mr. Sellinger had assured her the children were being well cared for. She'd trusted him.

She would not make that mistake again.

By the time James had moved their bags off the coach and up the stairs to their new accommodations, the sky was stained red and orange. Fontaine finally shook out of her paralysis and ushered the children up the narrow staircase one by one, feeling as if at any moment, a black-robed figure would appear out of the shadows and spirit them off to the mines. Only when all of them were inside with the door locked and bolted did she feel an ounce of relief.

The space was larger than appeared from outside, and Mrs. Wexford had provided them with cots and blankets, but as Fontaine drew open the sheer curtains on the only window, she cursed her lack of planning. She had been so determined to get to Halifax and sort out the communication issue that she had failed to consider the possibility that they would not be able to find lodgings.

An arm wrapped around her shoulders. Fontaine closed her eyes and leaned into Rosemary, not caring that the children and anyone outside could see them.

"We can't stay here long," Rosemary said.

"I know."

"Captain Charles said they'll be heading back to London in three days."

"I *know*," Fontaine said. She pressed her fists to her face. "You can leave. I can't. Not until I figure out what happened to them."

Rosemary squeezed her shoulder. "'Them'?"

The pressure on Fontaine's closed eyelids caused spectral shapes to appear in the darkness. The relocation scheme had been her idea. She was responsible for the fate of each of those souls. She couldn't leave Halifax without finding out what had happened to them, even if it meant missing the election. Even if it meant giving up on the foundation, the board, her dream of starting a boarding school.

The children had to come first.

"What about Peter, Quinn, Xavier, and Annie?" Rosemary asked.

A dull pounding started in Fontaine's head. "I brought them here. I'm responsible for them."

Rosemary rubbed small circles on her back. "We can't watch over them and investigate at the same time. There must be somewhere we could bring them. One of the city's orphanages?"

"No," Fontaine said. She shrugged off Rosemary's touch and faced the room. Xavier and Annie were arguing over the cots while Peter and Quinn shook out the sheets. None appeared to have heard their conversation, but she knew how they would react if they learned Rosemary wanted to dump them at an orphanage. Fontaine remembered cycling in and out of a dozen places as a child, the hope inside her dimming each time she'd escaped and had been caught and returned. She wouldn't put the orphans through that.

Not unless she had no other choice.

Rosemary gave a harsh exhale. "Well, if we're going to stay, we'll need more money. Is there anything we could sell?" She walked over to a bag in the corner of the room and opened it.

"I doubt it," Fontaine said. The swirling fabrics inside were hardly worth more than a few meals, assuming they could even find someone to buy them.

"What about this?" Rosemary asked, lifting a small box. "It's one of mine. A gold necklace."

"No," Fontaine said automatically. She felt guilty enough about dragging Rosemary across the ocean without having her offer to sell her possessions to support them.

Rosemary returned to Fontaine, grasped her hand, and placed the box in her palm. "Let me help."

The sincerity in her voice and the softness in her eyes made Fontaine's face grow hot. "Are you certain?"

Rosemary cupped her cheek. "You think I don't understand, but I do." She nodded toward Quinn and Peter, who were dragging their cots closer together. "Every time I look at them, I see my nieces and nephew. I'd prefer we leave them somewhere safe so we don't have to worry about them, but"—she sighed—"if they must stay with us, then I'll do whatever it takes to keep them safe."

Despite her words, the softness in Rosemary's eyes told Fontaine that she felt more for the children than she was willing to admit.

Chapter Twenty

THE DREARY MORNING had darkened to an even more gloomy afternoon by the time Fontaine had found a pawnbroker willing to give her a reasonable price for Rosemary's necklace. James had carted her and Xavier—the boy had insisted on joining her—through the streets for hours, refusing payment after learning they intended to investigate the snatchers. She might have insisted that he accept some form of remuneration, but Rosemary had reminded her before she'd left not to give up a single coin that she didn't have to.

"Just that?"

She looked up to find the pawnbroker, a short, heavy-set man with a wispy mustache and intense, brown eyes, staring at her expectantly.

"Yes," she said.

He gestured for her to follow. She had to duck beneath several suits hanging from the rafters before they reached an L-shaped desk squeezed between several tall stacks of crates. Xavier remained beside her in silence, his head turning around as he took in all the sparkling items that surrounded them.

"Put it here and I'll have a look," the pawnbroker said, taking a seat.

She placed the necklace down and slid it forward.

He picked the item up and moved his fingers along the chain until he had inspected every inch. Then he placed the necklace on a rusted scale and fidgeted with the dials until the scale balanced.

"Ten," he said.

It was more than she'd expected, but she had enough experience haggling that she was certain her surprise did not show on her face. "Thirty."

The man scowled. "Fifteen."

That he had gone up five dollars so quickly was a good sign. "Twenty."

The man grumbled but removed several bills from his pockets and slammed them on the table. As Fontaine gingerly picked them up, Xavier clutched her arm. She hadn't intended to take the boy with her, but he'd seemed so despondent in the attic. He was so quiet, so much so that the other children rarely spoke to him or involved him in their play.

She guided him out of the shop before the owner changed his mind, then down the street. They were within feet of James's carriage when a cart on the street broke, and the donkey leading it reared. She pressed herself to the outside of the nearest building, not wanting to be trampled, but Xavier darted into the chaos, so quick on his feet that he was gone before she could call him out to stop. When the dust settled, the boy had his arms around the neck of one of James's horses. The animal danced on its hooves, froth dripping from its mouth. It pulled Xavier off the ground but could not dislodge him.

"Come away from there, boy," James said. He tugged on his leads, but the wild horse continued to buck.

Xavier rubbed his face against the animal's hide. It stamped one hoof, shook its head, then settled.

Fontaine peeled herself away from the building and touched Xavier's shoulder. "That's enough." She didn't want James yelling at him again.

Xavier shook his head, not releasing his hold.

"Got a way with animals, do you, son?" James said, jumping down from his seat.

The boy tightened his grip.

Fontaine reached into her pocket and fingered the bills. They felt like hot coals burning a hole in her pocket. James had proven reliable, trustworthy, and hardworking. The moment he'd saved them from the docks, the idea of asking him to take on Xavier had flickered to life in her mind, but she'd held back, unsure of how he would receive the idea.

Perhaps now was the time.

She crouched down to Xavier's level. "Would you like to work with animals?"

He bobbed his head.

James grunted. "At least the boy is eager."

She straightened and faced the driver. "Are you seeking a new apprentice?"

He looked at the boy and frowned. "What have you got to offer as an apprentice price?"

She peeled two of the bills from her pocket, half of what she had earned from the sale, and held them toward the man. "This comes with the condition that you allow Xavier to write weekly letters confirming he is doing well."

It was the same condition she'd negotiated with Captain Charles regarding Winter. She would not make the mistake of handing off orphans to strangers without some manner of insurance again.

"A letter once a week." He nodded and took the bills. "It's a deal."

Then it was over. A simple matter, but it filled her with a glowing warmth. She had changed the course of the boy's life. In London, he might have been another limp body shoved into the gutter, then burned unceremoniously in a pit with hundreds of others. Now he might earn a living, perhaps raise children of his own.

This was why she couldn't give up. To the *ton*, the children living on the street were beneath their concern. She had to make them see they were wrong, that restoring each soul to a shining beacon of hope was as easy as dropping a few bills onto a plate.

Filled with renewed purpose, she grinned the entire trip back to the attic.

Chapter Twenty-One

ROSEMARY WALKED DOWN an alley between two houses, carrying a gently steaming basket that contained dinner for three children and two adults. The fragrant smell of onions and garlic made her mouth water, but she didn't dare open the basket before she reached her destination. Sampling the meat-filled pastries inside would leave her distracted. Vulnerable. Open to theft, if not any of the many things Fontaine had warned her about before she had left the attic. As the dowager baroness had spent a significant part of her life living on the street, Rosemary would not dismiss her warnings. She kept her senses attuned to the world around her, taking in the shush of leaves scattered by the wind and the rhythmic thump of her thin-soled shoes hitting the packed earth.

When she returned to the attic, she would have a serious conversation with Fontaine about the children. Finding a place for Xavier had been a stroke of good luck, but they could not afford the time or the cost in lodgings and food to continue to look after the others. As close as they had grown during the journey, they were only two women who had other tasks to accomplish. Despite that, Fontaine seemed intent on investigating the fire and figuring out what had happened to the children her foundation had shipped, all while keeping the orphans with them.

It wasn't that Rosemary didn't understand and even respect Fontaine's determination. The dowager baroness had suffered under the care of orphanages. But it would be much more efficient to leave the children in more capable hands. Rosemary had confirmed with several shopkeepers that Halifax was home to several organizations that specialized in caring for children. They couldn't *all* be bad.

She had to make Fontaine see sense because no matter what else happened in the coming days, they *would* be on the ship when it departed. Rosemary would see to that.

She turned a corner and a beam of sunlight peeked around the corner of a house, blinding her. She threw her hand in front of her face, then hurried forward until she was shielded by a derelict brick building.

The sound of leaves crunching beneath feet and whispered voices reached her.

She tightened her hold on the basket and increased her stride, even as her thighs burned in protest.

More whispering. A scattering of stones. A distant giggle.

Someone was following her.

Don't run, she thought. *Run and they'll know you as a victim.*

Fontaine had taught her that much. It was better to stand and face one's pursuers rather than flee. Confidence was often enough to chase away potential thieves.

She stopped, clutched her basket to her chest, and said in her most authoritative voice, "Reveal yourselves or cease following me. I am in no mood for games."

There was another shush of leaves flying around her heels. Then a group of three street urchins stepped out of the shadows and glared at her, a move more amusing than intimidating, as the children's heads only came up to her waist. It was hard to estimate their ages in the shadows, but she guessed they were between eight and ten.

One of the group, a skinny, black-haired waif garbed in a tattered, brown cloak, stepped forward and thrust her hand forward, palm up. "Hand o'er the basket."

There were three logical paths forward. One, she surrendered her baked goods to the obviously starving children and returned to the bakery for more. Two, she refused and hoped none of the children possessed a weapon. Three, she offered the food in exchange for something she wanted.

"This basket?" Rosemary asked. She lifted the cloth from the top, revealing a bounty of bread and pastries. She chose a chocolate éclair and bit into it, holding it carefully to avoid smearing chocolate over her gloves.

The children glanced at each other, hunger clear in the sharp lines of their cheekbones and the way they rocked from side to side, as if stopping themselves from launching at her. The leader gulped, then removed a stubby, wood-handled knife from inside her cloak and brandished it. "Hand it o'er!"

Rosemary finished the éclair and placed the basket on the ground. "I have a better idea. I would be willing to part with this basket for information. What's your name?"

The girl with the knife narrowed her eyes. "Jane. What kind of information? We ain't no snitches."

Rosemary pushed the basket forward slightly with her foot. "The Halifax Home for Destitute Children."

"Burn't," Jane said, her gaze on the basket. Her arm holding the knife trembled, as if she were unsure if she should continue to threaten or make a lunge for the prize.

"I know that." Rosemary said. "The newspapers said the only bodies recovered were adults. Did any of the children staying there survive? Where did they go? What about the owner, Mr. Sellinger?" With every question, she pushed the basket closer to the urchins. "Take this as an offering of good faith. You can find me at Mrs. Wexford's boarding house. When you bring me answers, I'll pay."

The sound of creaky wheels approaching caused two of the children to vanish.

"Deal," Jane said. She grabbed the basket and disappeared, just as a black cab rolled down the street at a slow pace, as if searching for a fare, although the residents of this neighborhood were not wealthy enough to do anything but walk to their destinations.

Before she could get a look at the driver, the man flicked his reins. The sleek, black horses before him leaped into a canter, and she had to stumble back to avoid the plume of dust that rose as the cab thundered past her. When she could see again without wincing, the vehicle was a black dot in the distance.

IT TOOK ROSEMARY another half hour to return to the bakery and purchase more food. By the time she made it back to the attic, her shins burned and her back twinged.

"Is this everything?" Fontaine asked as she accepted the basket.

"I encountered some difficulty on my way back," Rosemary said.

Fontaine handed off the basket to Annie to distribute to the others, then drew Rosemary outside and closed the door. "Tell me."

Rosemary described the group of children she had encountered, and the deal she had made with them. As she spoke, Fontaine's expression grew grimmer, and by the time Rosemary had finished, Fontaine was frowning and crossing her arms.

"What is it?" Rosemary asked. "Should I not have asked them to gather information for us?"

Fontaine sighed. "I don't know. Something doesn't seem right. Everyone we've spoken to seems to know children are being taken, but no one cares enough to do anything about it. They all know about the fire, but not how it started or why there were no children's bodies found in the wreckage of the Halifax Home. I don't understand what's happening." She rubbed her temples with her fingers. "We never should have come here. I should have listened to you."

Seeing Fontaine so miserable made Rosemary's heart ache. She put her hands on Fontaine's upper arms. "There is nothing we can do now but move forward." She started to pull the other woman into her arms when the sound of feet running upstairs made her step back and peer over the edge. A small figure was hurrying toward them. It was difficult to make out who it was, or if it was a boy or a girl, until the child rounded the last turn and stood on the steps, staring at them. It was the girl she'd spoken to in the alley, the leader of the small group. Jane.

"Got your in-fer-mation," the girl said, although she did not approach further.

"Is this…?" Fontaine whispered.

"Yes." Rosemary slid her hand into her pocket and removed a small coin purse. She offered it to the girl, who narrowed her eyes before darting forward and taking her payment. "Wait," she said, before Jane could run. "The information."

The girl looked over the edge of the stairs, as if judging how quickly she could descend. To Rosemary's relief, she seemed to decide facing the two adults was the better choice and made the purse vanish somewhere in her jacket before facing them with her hands in her pockets.

"Rumors say the fire was set," the girl said. "No accident. On account 'uv there's been lots 'uv coppers skulking about the place." She shoved her hands in her pockets. "Lots 'uv places have burnt."

"An arsonist," Rosemary whispered. "What kind of monster would try to murder a house full of orphans?"

"What about the children? Mr. Sellinger? His staff?" Fontaine asked. "Did any of them survive the fire? Where were they taken?"

Jane shuffled back a step. "Dunno about Mr. S and the rest, but none 'uv the young 'uns died. Those were shipped off to St. Mary's poorhouse." She glanced over her shoulder again.

"Can you take us there?" Fontaine asked.

Jane's eyes widened. "Take you lot? To St. Mary's?" She

snorted. "Mr. P won't never let proper folk like you inside."

The girl was, unfortunately, correct. Their apparel already did not match the neighborhood they were in. Rosemary had chosen her most drab outfit but had still noticed a fair number of people staring at her from the windows of the houses she'd passed on her trip to the bakery.

"What if I do it?" Annie asked.

Rosemary turned to find the girl closing the door to the attic. There were crumbs on her cheek. She scrubbed away with her sleeve.

"Absolutely not," Fontaine said. "It's too dangerous."

"What other choice do we have?" Rosemary asked. As much as she didn't want to put any of the children in danger, Fontaine's protectiveness was growing unreasonable. "We cannot lock the children in this room night and day."

Annie faced Fontaine with her back straight. "I'm brave and clever, just like you. Let me help."

Fontaine hiccupped on a sob, then closed her eyes and nodded.

Chapter Twenty-Two

ROSEMARY WATCHED FROM her vantage point in the alley as rail-thin creatures crept out of the poorhouse. Many were so emaciated that she could have knocked them over with a single finger, and all looked as poor as Quinn had been when they'd rescued him. For that reason, she was glad she had insisted Fontaine remain at the boarding house. She already felt such obvious guilt for her part in sending children to Halifax. She didn't need to see what had happened to them.

Rosemary grabbed the basket of cut dandelions that were part of her disguise as a flower seller and meandered out of the alley. With her dirt-smudged cheeks and bedraggled hair, no one gave her a second look. This was a necessity, as Jane the street urchin had insisted that the poorhouse had posted lookouts who would call an alarm if anyone who did not seem to belong to the neighborhood approached. Rosemary hadn't understood why until Fontaine and Annie had gently explained that it was often well-dressed strangers who came seeking what no one inside wanted to give up—especially the girls.

There was so much Rosemary didn't know about what it was like for street children. Every fact she learned further revealed a disturbing picture that she had avoided thinking about for most of her life. Her parents had taught her that the poor were nothing more than lazy, entitled scavengers, undeserving of help unless they showed proper gratitude and virtue, as well as a desire to better themselves through hard work. Even the children.

Standing in the alley dressed in rags, she had never felt the cruelty and injustice of that viewpoint more acutely. She had heard stories, of course, of sobbing mothers offering babies up for sale, but such stories were always exaggerated to elicit sympathy from potential donors, were they not?

For the first time, she looked around and saw not just the people walking along the streets, but the women and children sitting on the ground. The unfortunates whom she had always ignored, assuming that their condition had been of their own making.

When she returned to London, she would set aside as much of her monthly income as she could afford to go to charity. Saffron had been right all along. The poor of London deserved help as much as Annie and the other children.

She carefully checked the watch she'd tucked into her sleeve. According to their plan, Annie should've exited the poorhouse ten minutes ago. Fontaine had insisted the girl keep her head down and not act in any way that might draw attention. She was only to listen and watch, then report back after the allotted time had passed, even if she had learned nothing of value.

Finally, Annie darted out of the building, her face streaked with grease. She crossed the street and arrived at Rosemary's side.

"They're in there," Annie said, her face grim. "I saw Sam and Billy Smith, who used to hang around Barmy Park."

"How are they?" Rosemary asked, although a part of her didn't want to know. If the children exiting St. Mary's were any sign, many who had been sent from London had likely already perished. Fontaine would be devastated when she learned.

Annie dropped her gaze to her toes. "I won't lie. It's bad. 'Home children,' as they call them, aren't treated right. If any of them act up, a man comes and takes them to the Big House." She sniffed. "I tried to find out more, but they were all too scared to talk."

Rosemary wrapped an arm around her. "You did well."

As they turned out of the alleyway, a grungy-looking man in overalls stepped into their path. "Where would you be going, then?"

Rosemary drew herself upright. "Do not accost us, sir."

The man curled his lip. "This is none of your business, wench."

The insult was a slap across the face. She gaped at the man, her temper boiling inside her, until she remembered what she was wearing. Of course he didn't accord her any respect; he thought she was a flower seller.

The man grabbed Annie by the arm and dragged her, kicking and shrieking, out of the alley. Rosemary picked up a rock from the ground and rushed after them, prepared to do whatever it took to get Annie back, even if it meant bashing the man over the head. But when she met Annie's gaze, the girl shook her head back and forth rapidly, mouthing the word 'No.'

Rosemary stumbled and lost her grasp on the rock. It fell to the ground with a loud thump. Then the man and Annie were gone. Presumably he was returning her to the poorhouse, but Rosemary couldn't be sure. He could even be taking her to a brothel.

No.

She clasped her head in her hands. Annie had looked scared, but not terrified. She must have had some reason for stopping Rosemary from rescuing her. The right thing to do was return to Fontaine and tell her what had happened.

She stumbled out of the alley and dodged between men and women in fancy clothing until, at last, she was standing in front of the door to the attic. Fontaine opened the door at her knock.

"How did it go?" she asked, her hands clasped at her waist. Then she frowned. "Where is Annie?"

Guilt clotted in Rosemary's throat and made it difficult for her to speak. "Jane was right about St. Mary's." She quickly laid out what had happened to Annie. "They must have taken her back into the poorhouse."

Fontaine's face paled. "No. You're wrong."

A shiver went up Rosemary's arms. "What do you mean? Where else would they take her?"

"If it's anything like London, the poorhouse is where children who have no other uses are sent." Fontaine wrapped her arms around herself. "She's had more than a week of proper food, rest, and training. They'll see that and realize she'd be better off in service."

She had not considered that. If Fontaine was right and they sent Annie to become a maid, she might be in any house in the city. How were they going to find her? They didn't have time to wait for her to escape and find her way back.

Fontaine threaded her hands in her hair. "Annie said something to you about a house?"

"The Big House," a voice said.

Rosemary jumped. Jane stood in the doorway, having crept inside quietly.

"You lot want to help, right?" she asked.

Fontaine stared at her feet, blinking rapidly.

"Yes," Rosemary said. "Do you know where they took Annie?"

"I'll take you there," Jane said. "But you won't be let in looking like that." She grimaced. "The Big House is where the snatchers take their catches."

"So, they are connected," Fontaine whispered. Her expression hardened. "I'll go. I have a feeling I know what they're doing."

Rosemary wanted to ask what she meant, but the sharp edge to Fontaine's words and the way she clutched her arms around herself suggested she was in a fragile state. A determined, angry Fontaine was far preferable to a despondent one.

She took Fontaine's hand and looked at Jane.

"Take us there."

Chapter Twenty-Three

FONTAINE HELD HER chin high as she approached the entrance to the palatial building nestled among several similar structures in the heart of downtown Halifax. She could allow none of her nervousness to show. A dowager baroness, an earl's daughter, would not have been worried about what a businessman thought of her. She repeated her story in her head: She was preparing to open her new summer house outside Halifax and had come inquiring about servants. A local farmer had told her about the place. If she was right, someone was operating a business, kidnapping orphans and forcing them into indentured servitude. She'd seen such schemes before, although they were more often done under the pretense of charity. That only infuriated her more because it was a perversion of what the foundation was trying to do. Every child the foundation helped was provided with room and board during their education and then given a choice upon their graduation, even if that meant returning to the street.

As she climbed the steps to the entrance of the house, the door creaked open and a slip of a boy with huge, blue eyes peered out.

"I am here to see the master of the house," she said, although what she really wanted to do was fall to her knees and pull the poor child, who couldn't have been older than six, into her arms. He trembled as he clung to the door, hiding behind it like a shield.

"Have you recently taken up your post?" Fontaine asked softly. "Your butler should escort me to your receiving room."

The boy ducked his head and opened the door. When no other servant appeared, she followed him to a beautifully appointed room and perched on the edge of a green-upholstered sofa with her hands folded in her lap. Across from her, a tall-case clock ticked the seconds away, its brass face speckled with tiny rainbows cast by the sunlight reflecting off several glass orbs strung around the room. This, Fontaine was certain, was intentional. A grand first impression that left one dazzled before they met the owner of the house.

"Good afternoon," a deep voice said.

Fontaine forced herself to turn her head slowly and kept her head tilted upward. The man standing behind her was a match for the room in a well-tailored navy suit and ivory shirt. His hair was plastered tightly to his skull, except where it flowed across his cheeks into a bushy mustache.

She raised her hand and allowed him to take it and press his lips to her fingers.

"It is a pleasure to meet you," he said. "I'm John Prue."

His name sounded familiar, but she wasn't sure where she'd heard it before.

"Cynthia Fern," Fontaine said, deciding at the last second she didn't want this man knowing her real identity. There was something odd about him, something she couldn't place but set her on edge. Perhaps it was the intensity in his eyes or the way his lips quirked beneath his mustache in a smile that was almost a smirk.

He snapped his fingers, and the surrounding doors closed. "My housekeeper is arranging tea. Now what can I do for you, *Mrs. Fern?*"

He said her name with a peculiar inflection, as if he were rolling the words around in his mouth, savoring them as one might a fine wine. She reached for her fan and flicked it open to keep him from seeing how her hands trembled. A gently bred woman in her situation would not be nervous. She had wealth and power, both things Mr. Prue wanted.

"I've recently arrived from London," she said. "I thought to make a new start here, where the air is that much cleaner."

Mr. Prue tapped his fingers on the arm of his chair and nodded. But he was not so rude that he would rush her. That was good. She glanced at the clock. Barely a few minutes had passed. Not nearly enough time for Rosemary to have crept around to the back entrance of the house.

As if in answer to her prayers, the door creaked open and a young girl wearing the uniform of a maid entered, carrying a silver tray containing a tea set and a plate of biscuits. She crossed the room with rapid steps, porcelain cups rattling in their saucers.

Fontaine watched the girl carefully, searching for any trace of recognition that would identify the girl as hailing from London, but the maid kept her chin tucked to her chest as she placed the tray on a table in front of Mr. Prue. When she rose and started to turn, Mr. Prue snapped, and the girl froze.

"Serve us," Mr. Prue said. He gave Fontaine an apologetic smile. "I have the best girls trained in my own home."

The girl shook as she poured tea into their cups. It was a challenge for Fontaine to remain silent as Mr. Prue loudly criticized the girl's every move.

At last, he dismissed the maid. She bobbed a curtsey and scurried away.

Fontaine took her time blowing on her tea, then earned herself a few more seconds nibbling on a biscuit. Eventually, however, the tightening of the muscles in Mr. Prue's jaw told her she could delay no further.

"I have purchased a plot of land near the part of the river they call The Narrows," Fontaine said. "Do you know of it?"

"Yes," Mr. Prue said shortly.

"It might be several weeks before construction is complete, but I have not yet employed a butler or housekeeper to staff my new house. I was told it would be wise to seek you out at the soonest opportunity, as you offer the most competitive rates."

"I would agree with that assessment," he said the moment she'd stopped speaking.

"Then you can assist me?"

He chuckled. "You can set aside this fictional character you have created, Lady Kerry. I know why you are here."

Her hand holding her tea cup froze halfway to her lips. "Pardon?"

Mr. Prue lifted one thin eyebrow. "Did your companion not pass along my invitation on the S.S. *Great Arcadia*?"

Fontaine suddenly remembered where she'd heard Mr. Prue's name. It had been on the steamship during the crossing. Rosemary had told her that a man named Mr. Prue had wished them to join him for luncheon, but she had brushed off the request, too focused on seeing to the needs of the children.

"I-I apologize for the deception, Mr. Prue," Fontaine said. "I find that I am treated more fairly if I don't use my title. As for your invitation on the ship, I had prior commitments, but I..." She scrambled for an excuse but found none. To cover her lapse, she jerked her hand to the side and spilled her tea onto the carpet. "Oh, dear!" she cried. "I am terribly sorry."

He scowled, but in the next moment, several maids came rushing into the room to clean up the mess. These maids were even younger than the last. Perhaps Mr. Prue used his house to prepare the children for service, similar to how the foundation trained orphans in staging homes before shipping them to Halifax. That would explain why they kept their eyes downcast and worked with almost frantic urgency. Mr. Prue likely used the same harsh techniques to enforce obedience as London's workhouses.

When the mess had been cleared away and they'd moved to a different couch and chair that were not damp, she dabbed her lips with a handkerchief. "Terribly sorry. I am not quite myself. The trip from London was quite long."

"It is unfortunate to hear," he said. "Perhaps now we can

return to the true purpose of your visit." He sipped his tea. "I am well aware that you don't have the means with which to purchase a country home."

For the second time, her usual quick mind failed her. She sat with her mouth open, staring at him without a clue what to say next. He had seen straight through her plan and didn't seem in the least perturbed.

"No clever response?" he asked. His lips curved into a wicked grin. "Then I will speak for both of us, Lady Kerry. Or shall I call you 'Frannie'?"

His awful smile jostled her out of her frozen state. "No, you may not."

"You are so determined to paint me as a villain." He shook his head. "My lady, it was the operator of the Halifax home who approached me." He put his hand on his chest. "Mr. Sellinger was deep in debt and seeking a savior. If I had not stepped in, someone else would have. The children did not stop arriving, but Mr. Sellinger's actions meant there were no funds to care for them. *Something* had to be done with them. There were others who would have sent them back. I did them a favor by finding them gainful employment, even if it is not what you would consider respectable."

She ground her back teeth together. The man thought himself a hero. That should not have surprised her. Men like Mr. Prue rationalized their actions. She was sure he had not lost a single moment of sleep fretting over her choices, as she had.

"What about the children of Halifax?" she asked. "The 'snatchers'? Are you so desperate for workers that you're preying on the vulnerable within your own city?"

Mr. Prue scoffed. "Don't be ridiculous. Children go missing in every city. I would not have expected an educated woman such as yourself to believe such stories." He sniffed. "You should be thanking me. I have saved the lives of many that *your* foundation abandoned."

She winced. He was right. It was not as if she had any proof that the so-called 'snatchers' existed. The life of a street child was fraught with danger. She had only Jane's word that the snatchers took children to his house.

"Perhaps we should discuss what the future might look like," Mr. Prue said. "There is yet a way for you to achieve your goals, Lady Kerry."

"How?" she asked, although she was certain she wasn't going to like what he said next.

"By marrying me."

Her corset suddenly felt too tight. "What?"

He smiled. "I've surprised you again, I see. Allow me to explain." He cleared his throat. "I have established something of a reputation here. A reputation which has, so far, excluded me from the most exclusive events." He scowled. "The women of this city refuse me. But with you on my arm—"

"You would not become a baron if you married me," Fontaine said. If he thought to leverage her title, she would gladly disabuse him of that notion. Upon the death of her husband, she had inherited a mere pittance as a widow's portion.

He waved his hand. "This is not London, Lady Kerry. Titles matter little here. What I require is a charming, beautiful woman. A respectable wife. In exchange for your obedience and your silence regarding what you've discovered, I would allow you to take over correspondence to your precious foundation." He smoothed a hand over the front of his suit jacket. "Or you could leave, and I will ensure the foundation knows the full extent of the damage your relocation scheme has caused."

Although he had barely moved, she felt as if he had wrapped both hands around her throat and squeezed. "You wouldn't."

"I would write to every charitable organization in London, Lady Kerry. Every newspaper. You would never find another position. And that is just the beginning. Do you wish to know how many children have died in Halifax? I maintain a record of every death. You could visit their graves and beg for their forgiveness. I could take you to the charity hospital where the ones who've been injured while operating mining carts are recovering. What do you think they would say if I told them it was because of *you* they ended up here? Think of it, Lady Kerry. Think of how much they've suffered. You could undo all the damage you've done."

"I didn't..." Her voice died in her throat. She hadn't felt so helpless since she'd been a young girl. Mr. Prue was right. It was all her fault. The relocation scheme had been *her* idea.

"You could be my business partner," Mr. Prue said.

"Why would I want any part in your barbaric operation?"

His wicked smile returned. "Because I would allow you to make any decisions you wish regarding placement."

"Lies," she said, even as she imagined riding to the rescue of the children working in the mines and factories. She could save them from the awful situations she had caused them to be placed in. Assuming he was telling her the truth. A man like Mr. Prue would never allow his business to be uprooted so easily, not when it had resulted in wealth and power.

"So suspicious," Mr. Prue said. He shook his head. "You still don't understand. With you as my wife, I could secure investment for more profitable businesses."

There was a cruel logic to his words. By giving herself to him, she could save hundreds. It was a difficult offer to resist.

As if sensing she was close to agreeing, Mr. Prue put his hand over his heart. "You do not need to trust me. I would put this in writing. You would be protected by a contractual agreement."

Although she knew she should refuse him, she could imagine the partnership he described. The problem she'd faced in London had been a lack of funds. That was why she'd sought a position at a charitable foundation, because the wealthy men and women of the *ton* had refused to support the ventures of a woman with her past. But if she remarried in a place where no one remembered the newspaper articles that had slandered her reputation, perhaps things might be different.

She licked her lips. "What if...What if I wanted to open a

boarding school?"

Mr. Prue scowled. "There is no profit to be had in charity."

She gulped, then continued, choosing her words carefully. "The school could also accept students from wealthy families. If the best teachers were hired, the school would cultivate a reputation for excellence. Then we could offer free tuition for…others."

Mr. Prue ran a finger down the spine of his book. "I might be convinced. If you were a sufficiently respectful, dutiful wife."

A sour taste filled the back of her throat. A *dutiful wife*. There were so many ways she could interpret that phrase, and none of them were pleasant. But he was offering something she might never achieve in London. A chance to expand her influence and enact meaningful change.

All she had to do was marry him.

"What about the children who accompanied us from London, and Ro—my companion, Mrs. Summersby?" Fontaine asked, with a pang of guilt that it had taken her so long to consider how Rosemary would fit into the new life she was considering.

Mr. Prue made a show of pursing his lips and narrowing his eyes before shrugging. "The children can stay here until they find appropriate placements, and I see no reason you could not keep your companion. As long as you behave appropriately in public, what you do in private is of little concern to me."

The future stretched out before her. With Mr. Prue's wealth and influence, she would have every comfort. The children of Halifax would be free of their suffering. She could undo the damage she'd done and pay penance for her mistakes.

"What do you say?" Mr. Prue asked, wearing the smile of one who knew he had already won.

"I… I will consider it," Fontaine said in a small voice.

Chapter Twenty-Four

ROSEMARY STOOD AT the door to the Big House, her fretting escalated to panic. As much as she'd tried to reassure herself that Fontaine had been raised on the street and was therefore a resourceful woman, she couldn't help but feel that something was wrong. Had the owner of the house seen through Fontaine's act? Were there constables on their way, ready to cart Fontaine away for—what, exactly? Rosemary shook her head. She was being ridiculous. They had broken no laws. There had to be some other reason Fontaine was delayed.

She knocked on the door, and a small child with large, blue eyes opened it.

"Hello," she said. "I'm looking for—"

"I wondered how long it would take you to show up," a familiar voice said.

The child scurried away as the man who had asked about Fontaine on the S.S. *Great Arcadia* stepped out of the adjoining room into the hallway.

Mr. Prue.

He raised his arm, and Fontaine walked out of the same room and put her hand on his arm. When she met Rosemary's gaze, her eyes widened. She jerked away from Mr. Prue, but he held tightly, trapping her next to him.

"I'm sorry," Fontaine said. "I had to."

"What—" Rosemary started, before Mr. Prue spoke over her.

"I am pleased to inform you that your employer has agreed to be my wife."

Each word was a dagger in her heart.

"Of course, the orphans you've been accompanying are welcome to stay until the wedding," Mr. Prue continued. He snapped his fingers, and an older woman in a black gown appeared. She kept her head tilted to the floor and her hands clasped at her waist.

"See Lady Kerry and her companion to the diamond suite, Mrs. Feather," Mr. Prue said. "And have their possessions transported here from wherever they were staying before." He released Fontaine and walked toward Rosemary. The malice shining out of his face made her shiver.

"I trust you will enjoy your stay," he said.

Then he exited the house.

The moment the door closed behind him, Rosemary rushed toward Fontaine and took her hands. "What did he do to you?" She could not imagine Fontaine agreeing to a marriage unless Mr. Prue had backed her into a corner.

A tear trailed down Fontaine's cheek. Rosemary cupped the other woman's face in her hands, even as Mrs. Feather stood patiently beside them. Rosemary didn't care. Fontaine was hurting, and it was Mr. Prue's fault.

"Not here," Fontaine whispered. She took a step back and dashed her tears away.

Rosemary longed to close the distance between them with every inch of her being, but she would not go against Fontaine's wishes.

Mrs. Feather silently led them up three flights of stairs, then down a hallway to an open door. When Rosemary stepped inside, she hissed in a breath. Every piece of furniture was covered in gilded gold, from the four-poster bed to the dressing table. Even the frames surrounding the large, circular windows overlooking the back of the house sparkled with gold dust.

"So, this is to be my gilded cage," Fontaine said. She drifted over to the enormous bed and thumped onto it.

"What happened?" Rosemary asked. She joined Fontaine on the bed, putting her arm around the other woman's shoulders. Unlike when Mr. Prue had done the same, Fontaine didn't cringe away from her touch, but leaned into her. Tears streamed down her cheeks, and her jaw trembled.

"Did he threaten you?" Rosemary asked. "I don't know the laws here, but I am sure he cannot compel you to marry him."

Fontaine hiccupped a laugh. "He didn't threaten me. He wants me to oversee his business."

A gnawing sensation started in Rosemary's stomach, as if she hadn't eaten in days. "And you believed him?"

"I could make a real difference. Don't you understand? There's so much suffering here and I'm to blame for much of it. I owe the orphans in this city a debt that I'll never be able to repay." She looked at Rosemary with tear-filled eyes. "He said you could stay with me. We can still be together."

Rosemary wanted to take Fontaine's shoulders and shake her. "You made a mistake. That doesn't mean you should have to throw yourself on his sword. We can go back to London, and you can tell the foundation everything."

Fontaine shook her head. "I can't abandon the children who are already here."

Rosemary gritted her teeth. "Have you already accepted Mr. Prue's offer?"

"I told him I'd consider it," Fontaine said. "But he knows as well as you I'm going to say *yes*. What else can I say?"

"Anything but that!" Rosemary shouted. "How could you give in so easily? What happened to investigating? Bringing the snatchers to justice?"

Fontaine dabbed her eyes with a handkerchief but didn't respond. That somehow only made Rosemary angrier. The determined, passionate woman she cared for had vanished inside the miserable, guilt-ridden creature sitting in front of her.

"Fine. Give up," Rosemary said. "But don't expect me to help you or stay. Married women don't need *companions*."

Chapter Twenty-Five

FONTAINE NODDED AND smiled as well-dressed strangers chatted about which lady had worn a gown of last year's fashion to Mrs. Tallow's garden party, or which gentleman had been kicked out of a gambling house for starting a drunken fight. Matters she could not have cared less about but were the pinnacle of importance to these people.

"Who made your lovely gown, Lady Kerry?" a woman wearing a fortune of rubies and diamonds asked. "I am looking for a new modiste. My current one"—she plucked at the fine, knotted, cream lace decorating her bodice—"has not met my expectations."

Fontaine murmured something appropriate, as it was clear the woman did not actually want her to answer the question. She was making a statement to redirect the conversation to herself.

Halifax society, as far as Fontaine could tell, was nearly identical to that of London with fewer titles but no fewer people thinking themselves to be of great importance. The vain, fluttering members of the *ton* cared only about themselves. They might occasionally summon an ounce of empathy to raise funds for a faraway cause, while ignoring the suffering going on a block from their homes. But even that would be to make themselves feel magnanimous.

If the previous week had not already proven it, this event of Mr. Prue's had confirmed for Fontaine that she didn't belong in society. Regardless of her parentage, she had raised herself in an environment wherein one's chosen family had been more important than one's blood relatives.

Except she'd pushed her chosen family away.

A tear dripped down her cheek. She quickly dashed it away. Rosemary simply couldn't understand the pressure she was under. She had tried doing everything herself. She had tried offloading work to others to act in her place. She had tried *everything*, but no matter what she did, children suffered. Mr. Prue was right. It made more sense for her to operate in the shadows, where she could do more good.

The musicians in the corner of the room started up a country dance that Fontaine didn't recognize. Rather than allow one of the well-dressed gentlemen to escort her onto the dance floor, she begged a megrim and retreated to a corner to watch. Mr. Prue had finally left her alone, and she would enjoy every moment not in his company.

"Lady Kerry?" a male voice asked.

Fontaine turned to face the man who had approached her. It took a moment for her to recall his name from when Mr. Prue had introduced her earlier that evening. Rowan Martin. He wore the same black suit, vest, and trousers as most of Mr. Prue's guests. The only thing that set him apart was the thick, curly beard that covered the bottom half of his face and most of his bulbous nose.

"I apologize, but I do not feel like dancing," she said. It was rude, and it would have earned her a cut in London, but Mr. Martin only smiled, or so she assumed. She could not see his mouth, but his pale-green eyes crinkled at the edges.

"That is not what I wished to speak to you about, Lady Kerry," he said. He looked around the room, then continued in a quieter voice. "Mr. Prue mentioned you are to take over his operation?"

So, her future husband was already creating a reputation for her. She straightened. Here was a chance to undo some of the harm he had caused.

"I am indeed, and I can assure you my first action will be to remove children from inappropriate placements."

Mr. Martin stared at her, wide-eyed, for a few seconds before clapping his hands together. "Excellent!"

Her jaw dropped open.

"I'd be pleased if you would tell me more about your plans," he continued. "I have long had issue with Mr. Prue's operation."

She had to blink several times before she realized he was not at all the same as the other men present. "I-I had intended to start a boarding school," she said. When Mr. Martin didn't scoff or dismiss her, she continued. "A place for the poor to earn the skills needed to take up a trade." She didn't know why she was telling Mr. Martin so much. The words seemed to pour out of her.

"Lady Kerry, I cannot say how pleased I am to hear this," Mr. Martin said. "My wife will be similarly pleased."

"Mrs. Martin did not accompany you?"

She did not remember being introduced to such a lady, and any woman who was interested in charitable ventures was someone with whom Fontaine wanted to become more acquainted.

Mr. Martin shook his head. "She does not approve of Mr. Prue."

Even better. If Mr. Prue required her to maintain a presence in Halifax society, she would need allies.

"I would love to speak more," she said before spotting Mr. Prue heading her way. "Perhaps Mrs. Martin might join me for afternoon tea next week?"

She barely had time to hear Mr. Martin's agreement before Mr. Prue reached them.

"Mr. Martin, if you might excuse us, I need to take my future bride away," he said before Mr. Martin could do more than say a word in response, leading Fontaine onto the dance floor. "Where is your darling companion, Mrs. Summersby?" he asked. "It is only proper that she remains at your side when you are not with me." He squeezed her hand to the point of pain, making her shudder.

"She was… not feeling well," she said.

He huffed. "Well. In any case, I don't want you associating with Mr. Martin."

"Why?" She attempted to put some distance between them, but Mr. Prue drew her tighter to his side.

"I only invited him because Halifax society is quite small. There are more useful connections you might form," he said. "A *dutiful wife* would do well to abide by my requests."

She bit the inside of her cheek to keep from responding. Instead, she spent a few seconds imagining what her life would be like if she were to cultivate a new life here, without Mr. Prue. If Mr. Martin was any sign, she might be able to gather sponsors whose support would allow her to open her boarding school on her own.

The temptation was strong, but there were too many ways such a path could go wrong. Most importantly, Mr. Prue was a man, and she was a woman. Even in Halifax, far away from the scandals that had tarnished her name, she had little chance of winning in a direct confrontation against him. Especially if anyone discovered the true nature of her relationship with Rosemary. Halifax society was no less judgmental than the *ton*.

No, as lovely as the idea was, she had already given her commitment to Mr. Prue. She would be married again, even if it meant breaking her heart.

HOURS LATER, AFTER suffering through an entire evening of smiling and dancing, Fontaine sat in front of her dressing table, turning a suspicion around in her mind. The possessive way Mr. Prue had led her around the room that evening made her wonder if he would really allow Rosemary to remain living with them.

She would have to ensure that was put in writing. Then again, she didn't know if Rosemary even wanted to stay with her. They hadn't spoken since the fight. Neither had she seen Peter or Quinn, although Mr. Prue assured her that they were well and that she would be allowed to see them as soon as he and Fontaine were wed.

She put down her brush and closed her eyes. She couldn't give in to despair. Not yet. She still had her wedding night to endure. It wasn't as if she hadn't had sex with a man before, if only the one. She had even occasionally enjoyed the experience with Malcom. But thinking about Mr. Prue's sweaty, grunting form crouched atop her made her shudder. She would rather spend another night curled up against Rosemary's side. More than once, she'd wished that Mr. Prue's home was smaller. Then she might've been forced to share a room with Rosemary as they had on the ship, even if she wasn't sure the woman would invite her touch.

Fontaine rose and realized the door to her soon-to-be husband's room was open. That was likely his doing, ensuring she was reminded of what would come after their wedding. She rose and entered his chamber. It would be better to get used to her new situation, so there would be less chance that she would balk when the time came.

She aimlessly strolled to his desk and picked up an unfinished letter he had been writing. She expected it to be more tiresome business, but her eyes stumbled upon a phrase that made her pause. Rather than return to her room, she lit a candle with a match from a box on his desk, then held the flame close to the paper. With each word that she read, the sour taste in her mouth intensified, until she felt she might cast up her accounts all over his desk.

Mr. Prue had written to Mr. Blake with instructions that more children should be sent to Halifax at the earliest opportunity, and that Mr. Blake should inform the board that all the children had been placed in excellent situations. He also included a note specifically for Mr. Hill, confirming the foundation would receive its portion of the funds collected on schedule.

She shoved the paper aside and rifled through Mr. Prue's desk until she found another letter, a response from Mr. Blake telling Mr. Prue of her impending arrival in London.

He had known she was coming.

The next sheet in the stack tallied the amount of money Mr. Prue was gathering for each child. He had not simply placed the orphans into mines and factories—he was *leasing* the children, gathering part of their income, ostensibly to save it until they were older, but she doubted he had any intention of returning the money to the children.

But the last item of correspondence was the worst. In the letter, again addressed to Mr. Blake, Mr. Prue advised that the volume of children did not meet the demand in Halifax. If Mr. Blake could not gather children from orphanages or workhouses, Mr. Prue wrote, perhaps there were other avenues they might explore.

It was so much worse than Fontaine had realized. He was not only responsible for the 'snatchers' whom he had mocked her for believing in, but he was actively stealing children from the streets of London, too. That explained his connection to the Whitechapel workhouse.

She put his desk back in order, resisting the urge to spit upon his beautifully polished mahogany chair, and returned to her room. She had to find Rosemary and tell her everything that had happened. Then they could figure out what to do next because she no longer had any intention of marrying Mr. Prue. Unfortunately, neither could they sneak out in the dead of night without revealing what she had learned. She had to continue exactly as she had, lest he grow suspicious.

She pulled the rope in her room to summon a servant, but when the door opened a few moments later, it was Annie who appeared, dressed in the uniform of a maid. It was only Mrs. Feather, standing in the hallway behind Annie, that stopped

Fontaine from crying out with joy. Mr. Prue's housekeeper crossed over her chest and watched Annie with narrowed eyes.

"How may I help you, my lady?" Annie asked. When Fontaine met her gaze, she winked.

Was it possible that Mr. Prue hadn't realized Annie had been one of the children they'd transported from London? The orphans had stayed out of sight of the guests on the ship, and Mr. Prue had only told her that 'the children' had been moved from the boardinghouse. He hadn't mentioned Peter's or Quinn's names or specified how *many* children.

Fontaine blew out a breath and smiled. "Please summon my companion."

They had much to discuss.

Chapter Twenty-Six

T HREE WEEKS AGO, Rosemary had been certain that her world was big enough with only the people she cared about in it. She had willfully ignored the concerns of the people living outside her carefully cultivated bubble and had even scoffed at Saffron's dedication to charity. It was hard to believe that her entire perspective had changed in such a short time, and all because of a single person.

Her eyes and throat ached from resisting the tears that threatened to come whenever she thought of Fontaine. She had carefully avoided her since the dowager baroness had told her she wouldn't give up her plan to marry Mr. Prue.

She had expected it to be difficult to avoid Fontaine, but Mrs. Feather had seemed almost smug when Rosemary had asked to have her meals brought to her room. This was in stark contrast to the chilly response she'd received when she'd asked about Peter and Quinn. Mrs. Feather would only tell her the boys were being looked after, and Rosemary's own attempts to question the servants and search the house had yielded no clues.

She would find them. She just needed more time.

But if she was going to stay at Fontaine's side, then Saffron and Angelica needed to know why she wasn't returning, at least not right away.

A drop of liquid fell on her letter, blurring her carefully written words. She scowled and brushed the tears from her cheeks.

She was far too old to be weeping over something so insignificant as missing her nieces. It wasn't as if she would never see them again. There were regular ships traveling between London and Halifax. She just couldn't leave Fontaine while there was still a chance she could be convinced that she was making a mistake.

She crumpled her half-written missive into a ball and tossed it into the fireplace, then selected a fresh piece of paper and started again. She would complete the letter, even if it took her all night.

A rap at the door provided a welcome distraction. When she opened it, Annie stood in the doorway.

"Shh," Annie said. She darted her eyes to the side, then dipped her head.

Rosemary leaned out the door and spotted Mrs. Feather at the end of the hall. The woman appeared to be speaking to another maid but cast several glances toward Annie.

So, Mr. Prue didn't know that Annie had come with them. That was an interesting development. Hopefully, one they could use to their advantage.

"Lady Kerry wishes to speak with you, madam," Annie said.

At Fontaine's title, Rosemary's heart gave a lurch. She was tempted to say *no* because she feared she would erupt into tears the moment she saw Fontaine, that all of her reluctance would melt away and she'd throw herself into Fontaine's arms and agree to do anything she wanted.

"I'll see her shortly," Rosemary said. Then she closed the door and rushed to her mirror, checking her complexion and the fit of her gown. It was silly. She felt as if she was a young girl preparing to meet a suitor, not going to meet a woman she had already shared a bed with.

One final curl tucked into place, a fresh handkerchief tucked into her sleeve, and she set out, her footfalls silent on the lush, scarlet carpet of the hallway. Several flights of stairs and what seemed like an impossibly long hallway later, she reached Fontaine's door and rapped on it softly. Perhaps if Fontaine didn't hear, Rosemary could pretend that she was not inside and return to her room, avoiding the inevitable confrontation.

The door creaked open, and Fontaine's face peered out. Her eyes were bloodshot, her nose bright red.

"Come in," Fontaine said, her voice thick. She turned and walked toward the bed.

Rosemary stepped inside and allowed the door to close behind her. She wasn't sure what she had expected, but it was certainly not what was presented before her. A breeze flowed in through an open window, rifling sheets of paper splayed over the writing desk. The adjoining door was blocked by a table, as if Fontaine were worried that someone would force their way in.

"It's Mr. Prue," Fontaine said. She thumped down on the bed.

Rosemary came to sit beside her. "What do you mean?"

"It's been him all along. Here, and in London. I can't believe I didn't realize it sooner." Fontaine's shoulders curled inward. "What have I done?"

That was more than Rosemary could bear. She tugged Fontaine into her arms as the dowager baroness gave great, gulping sobs.

"You don't have to marry him," Rosemary said as she rubbed Fontaine's shuddering back. "We'll figure out some other way to help the orphans who are already here."

Fontaine gave a hiccupping laugh, then pushed away and shook her head. "I have no intention of marrying Mr. Prue. Not after what I discovered." She rose and shuffled over to a table. She picked up a sheet of paper and brought it back. "Read this."

"A letter?" Rosemary asked as she took the sheet. The wax seal was still hanging off the edge. She skimmed through it, her throat tightening with each sentence. No wonder Fontaine was upset. Mr. Prue was more than a simple businessman. He was a criminal of the worst sort.

"He's taking them by force from London," Fontaine said. "He earns a monthly fee for each child he places." She dashed her tears away with her sleeve. "They're like cattle to him. The letters claim he keeps part of the fee for the children when they come of age, but…"

"There's no way he'll give any of it up," Rosemary finished. She handed the letter back to Fontaine before she gave into the urge to crumple it into a ball. "Blackguard."

The letter also explained several other things.

"Mr. Blake has been following us," she said.

Fontaine's head jerked up. "What?"

Rosemary counted out the clues on her fingers. "The carriage that followed us after we left the Whitechapel workhouse. Then again, as we were departing. And maybe a few days ago when I met Jane in the alley." She bit the inside of her cheek before adding, "I thought I saw him on the ship, as well. I didn't tell you because I wasn't sure. But now I'm certain. Mr. Blake has been following us. He's probably working for Mr. Prue."

"What are we going to do?" Fontaine asked, her voice cracking.

Rosemary squeezed her close. "We're going to stop him."

Chapter Twenty-Seven

"I'M SORRY," FONTAINE said. "You were right, but I was so sick with guilt that I almost made a terrible mistake."

She felt as if her body would crumble at the slightest touch. How could she make up for the damage she had caused? She was mortified that she had not seen through Mr. Prue's scheme. If she hadn't thought to explore his room, she might not have learned about his treachery until it had been too late.

It was still possible for her to lock him into his promises with carefully drafted contracts, but she could no longer stomach the idea of submitting to him, even if it meant she could save so many children. She would be of no value to anyone if she couldn't leave her bed because she was so disgusted with herself.

"It's not your fault," Rosemary said.

Fontaine snorted. "It absolutely is. If I hadn't been blinded by my desperate need to make up for my failure, I might have seen what was right under my nose." She let out a long breath as the realization settled over her. "I've never felt like I belonged in society. I was born on the streets. When my father found me, I was angry for a long time. My half-siblings and stepmother despised me, and I felt like I couldn't do anything right. When I finally accepted my fate, I… I felt so guilty." She put her face in her hands, unable to bear the look of sympathy on Rosemary's face. "What makes me, the bastard daughter of a wealthy man, entitled to wealth? How am I different from Annie and the others? They deserve everything I have."

Her shoulders shook. Rosemary grabbed her hands and drew them away from her face. She slid off the bed and knelt between Fontaine's legs, a position which gave Fontaine an ample view of creamy skin decorated with delicate lace. She averted her gaze.

"Don't," Rosemary said as she cupped Fontaine's cheeks in her hands. "Don't deny yourself." Then she brought their lips together.

A bolt of pure lust shot through Fontaine, and she wrapped her arms around Rosemary. She tilted her head, allowing the other woman better access, then moaned deep in her throat.

God, how she had wanted this. She had dreamed of kissing Rosemary every night since they had shared a bed. A vision of what might happen next flashed through her mind in quick snippets and made dampness flow to her sex.

Rosemary pushed her back until she was pressed to the bed, then leaned over her. She kissed a trail from Fontaine's lips down to the neckline of her gown, then followed that line until she reached Fontaine's shoulder.

"You are wearing far too many clothes," Rosemary said.

Fontaine wriggled out of Rosemary's embrace and clawed at her back for the strings that would release her from the tight clasp of her gown. When she'd grasped them, she tugged so hard that one shoulder of her gown popped free, but the other remained stuck.

With a hearty laugh, Rosemary swatted Fontaine's hands away, then carefully, lovingly, undid the strings until both of her shoulders were free.

"Too slow," Fontaine said. She shoved out of her gown, kicking it away until it lay in a crumpled heap. When she turned around, Rosemary had done the same.

They came together again, hands and lips finding each other. Rosemary's tongue slipped inside of Fontaine's mouth. The faint taste of brandy was intoxicating, but she wanted that mouth on other parts of her, especially between her legs, where her sex throbbed with *need*.

Hands came around Fontaine's back, but there was still too much fabric. She reached for Rosemary's waist and untied the strings of her petticoats, which slipped down to puddle at their feet. Rosemary did the same to her. Then they were left in only their corsets and shifts. The clasps on the front of each garment made it easy for them to shed, and then they were pressing their breasts to each other, with only their shifts separating them.

The hard buds of Rosemary's nipples pressed into her chest, and Rosemary's lips were soft beneath hers.

She reached down and lifted her shift over her head. Rosemary fell to her knees and trailed hot, open-mouthed kisses down her chest, then her stomach, and finally her hips.

"The bed," Rosemary whispered against her sex. The words made her insides clench. She crawled onto the bed and lay on her back. Rosemary tore viciously at her hair, sending pins flying. Thick, wavy locks tumbled free and formed a curtain around her body.

It was the most seductive thing Fontaine had ever seen. She squeezed her thighs together.

Rosemary crawled onto the bed on her hands and knees, her long hair draped over her shoulders, her breasts hanging heavily, nipples taught. She smoothed her palms down Fontaine's sides until both hands cupped her hips. She squeezed, then dropped her head and kissed Fontaine's sex. It was barely a brush of lips but made her back arch. She tried to buck her hips, but Rosemary pressed her down.

"Impatient," Rosemary whispered. Then she removed one hand and slid her index finger up and down Fontaine's slit, slowly increasing the pressure until at last she curled her fingers and slid them between the folds of Fontaine's vulva, rubbing her there, coming closer and closer, but not quite…

Rosemary pressed her mouth around Fontaine's clitoris and sucked. She slid one, then a second finger, inside. The things she was doing with her mouth and her tongue made Fontaine squirm. The coil inside her tightened ever so slowly. Too slowly. Fontaine clenched her muscles of her abdomen.

"Relax," Rosemary whispered. "Let it come slowly."

Fontaine grumbled but obligingly released her muscles. The ebb and flow of her pleasure came in slow waves until at last she burst apart. The orgasm traveled from her center all the way to the top of her head. She had never felt such intense pleasure and savored every moment until she was left boneless with relief.

ROSEMARY FELL ONTO her back, more satisfied than she'd been in years. She turned on her side, ready to wrap her arms around Fontaine, but the other woman was already wriggling down the bed.

So that was how it was to be.

A shiver of anticipation rushed through her. She had dreamed of having Fontaine's lips and hands on her since they had shared the night on the ship. She had never expected to experience that pleasure again, had nearly convinced herself that it had been a dream.

"What do you like?" Fontaine asked. She put her hands on Rosemary's thighs and smoothed her palms up and down.

"Rough," Rosemary said. "I like it rough. You don't have to hold back."

Fontaine's lips quirked. "You're sure about that?"

Rosemary gulped. She would've never dared to utter those words to any man. They would have taken her predilection for pain as permission to enact all manner of awful things upon her. It was not something she had shared with most of her partners, instead choosing to pretend she had come to orgasm rather than subject them to the level of torment they needed to inflict to bring her to a similar state. But Fontaine was different. Rosemary knew she would not go too far.

Fontaine dipped her head and rasped her tongue deep into Rosemary's sex. It wasn't enough pressure, but the action itself was so unexpected that she gasped. Then Fontaine dug her nails into Rosemary's thigh and drew them down, while swirling her tongue around Rosemary's clitoris.

The pain, which might've made her yelp in other circumstances, transformed into a burst of fiery pleasure. Fontaine seemed to know exactly how hard to push. There would be white lines along Rosemary's flesh when they finished, but nothing more.

Nothing permanent.

Fontaine pressed Rosemary's entrance wide, then slid fingers inside one at a time until Rosemary was so full that she had to hold herself back from squirming under the pressure. She closed her eyes as the action of Fontaine's tongue upon her clitoris and the fingers not quite thrusting, but curling inside her, seeking that secret spot that would send her over the edge, brought her close to orgasm. It hovered over her like a skittish animal, ready to bolt if she lost her focus. But she did as she had bidden Fontaine and forced her muscles to relax.

"I'm close," she whispered. "Don't stop."

Fontaine used her other hand to draw her nails down Rosemary's back, and that was it. The orgasm tore through her, a conflagration of sharp sensation that made her toes curl.

Fontaine slowed her motions. That was another thing Rosemary appreciated about having women as partners. They knew to draw out the pleasure rather than stop completely. Nothing was more of a shock to a system than to go from intense pleasure to nothing. It quite ruined the orgasm. As did remaining at an intense frequency. Fontaine seemed to know exactly when the pleasure faded.

Chapter Twenty-Eight

FONTAINE SLID OUT of Rosemary's arms. As much as she wanted to cuddle and forget everything that had happened over the past few days, there was something she had to do, and she suspected Rosemary would disapprove.

She tiptoed through the room, donning her clothing piece by piece. Her hair was a hopeless mess, so she tied it up as best she could and shoved it beneath a bonnet. She would have a maid sort it out when she returned.

A candleholder sat on her writing desk. She picked it up and exited the room on soft feet, closing the door behind her so slowly that it did not creak. Then she pulled a match out of her pocket and lit the candle. The narrow hallway stretched long in front of her, disappearing into a dark void. The only sounds in the house were the occasional creak above her and the tick of a clock somewhere in the distance.

When she reached the library, the door was partially open. A gentle glow emanated from inside. As she had expected, Mr. Prue was still awake. He kept unusually late hours, sleeping well past breakfast. She had imagined that might have been to her benefit, when she had considered becoming his wife. It would have allowed her to accomplish her tasks while leaving as little time as possible for them to be alone.

She pushed the door open. Mr. Prue sat on a chair with a leatherbound book in his hands. As she entered, he lowered the book.

"Lady Kerry. It is late for you to be about."

She closed the door behind her. "I know what you've been doing."

Mr. Prue gently set his book on the table beside him. "Come, let us discuss."

She ground her back teeth together. "Did you hear what I said?"

Mr. Prue folded his hands in his lap. "Of course."

"I know that you have been corresponding with Mr. Blake," she said. "You're not just profiting from the exploitation of orphans. You're *taking* children, both here and in London."

Mr. Prue removed a pipe and a small bag from the drawer of the desk beside him. "That is correct."

She stared as he prepared his pipe, shoving a wad of tobacco into the flared end of the smooth pipe before lighting a match to set it smoking.

"You admit it, then?" Fontaine asked.

Mr. Prue puffed on his cigar several times before answering. "I suspected you might discover what I have been doing." He blew out a large cloud of smoke. "What do you intend to do now?"

She shuffled her feet to keep from stomping. The man was infuriating. "I will not be the wife of a man in the business of kidnapping children."

"I rather think you will," Mr. Prue said. Then he rose from his seat and walked over to the long cord in the corner of the room. He tugged it once before returning to his seat. He had barely resumed his position when the door behind Fontaine opened, and Mrs. Feather stepped inside.

"Is there something you require, sir?" she asked.

"Bring the children," Mr. Prue said.

Fontaine clenched her hands. This conversation was not going the way she had expected. Rather than balk or shout at her, Mr. Prue acted as if this had been his plan all along.

"I intended to let them go after we married," Mr. Prue said. "But you have left me no choice."

The door creaked open again, and Mrs. Feather returned, clasping a red-faced Peter's upper arm in her grip. Annie stood beside the housekeeper, holding Quinn in a similar manner, although the look on Quinn's face suggested he had not been handled as roughly as his brother.

That meant Annie had yet to be discovered.

Fontaine carefully avoided her gaze. While Annie remained undetected, there was a chance she could help them.

"These boys must be quite important to you," Mr. Prue said. He spent a leisurely moment puffing on his pipe. Every tick of the clock increased the tightness in Fontaine's chest until she was certain she would scream.

"You wouldn't want anything bad to happen to them, would you?" Mr. Prue asked. "There are plenty of places in Halifax that would welcome such beautiful children. Places a child would never be able to leave."

Fontaine felt as if someone had scooped her insides out and scorched what was left. She could not allow him to hurt Peter and Quinn. Even if sending them to a terrible fate meant she could save dozens or hundreds more children, she couldn't do it. The boys had been through too much already.

"Don't do this," she whispered.

He examined the end of his pipe as if it were the most interesting thing in the room. "You know, I wasn't lying when I told you Mr. Sellinger reached out to me about more funds. He insisted that I continue the operation as he had arranged it, even though it was hardly profitable. So, I wrote to some colleagues of mine here and explained about our *disagreement*." He chuckled. "Old buildings are so very prone to fire."

She wanted to slap her palms over her ears and scream at him to stop, but her muscles refused to move.

"At least all the children escaped," Mr. Prue continued. "I believe the door leading to the staff's quarters was found to have jammed and the staff was trapped. As I had not yet found a supplier to replace the old windows, they couldn't escape through them, either."

"Murderer," she whispered.

Mr. Prue shrugged. "Call me whatever you want. I expect you to go happily into our marriage. I will give you exactly what I have promised, but I will not tolerate misbehavior. So long as you accomplish your responsibilities as my wife…" He waved his hand. "You can use the rest of your time as you wish."

At least she would not be left with nothing.

"And Rosemary?" Fontaine asked.

Mr. Prue's eyes narrowed. "You cannot have everything you want, Lady Kerry. You have betrayed me, and I know it was Mrs. Summersby who led you to it. No, you might have once enjoyed the companionship of your friend, but no longer. Mrs. Summersby will return to London on the next available ship. And do not think I would make it so easy for you to sever our arrangement. If you betray me again, I will ensure that you regret it."

Her heart plummeted. She knew what Rosemary would say. She would claim Fontaine was being soft-hearted, that she could not protect every child by herself. Mr. Prue could simply cast Quinn and Peter aside and grab others to take their place. There had to be a point where she said *no*.

She dipped her head, carefully avoiding meeting Annie's gaze. For now, she must play the beaten-down woman and allow Mr. Prue to believe he had won.

"Much better," Mr. Prue said. "See? That wasn't so difficult. You will make a lovely wife."

Swallowing her instinctual response to that crooning statement was more difficult than she'd expected.

Chapter Twenty-Nine

I F SOMEONE HAD asked Rosemary what she'd expected to be doing in Halifax when they'd been on the steamship, the answer would most certainly not have been 'attending a ball.' Yet that was exactly where she found herself, standing next to a window in Mr. Prue's ballroom, dressed in a hideous yellow-and-orange-printed cotton dress. The boning in the bodice dug into her stomach and the hem was several inches too short, but the manner with which Mrs. Feather had delivered the garment to her room that afternoon had implied that it was not a generous gift from Mr. Prue, but a requirement to be allowed to attend. Considering what Fontaine had told her, that he'd threatened the twins and demanded Rosemary return to London on the next available transport, she'd decided not to fight him on a simple matter of wardrobe.

She'd argued with Fontaine about how easily she'd given up, but Mr. Prue's threats seemed to have broken something inside Fontaine. In contrast, Rosemary was more determined than ever to spend the little time she had before Mr. Prue sent her away trying to find a way to stop him.

She clung to the shadows, her gaze never leaving Fontaine. If the difference in their social status had been obvious before, now it was glaring. Fontaine's golden, silk gown sparkled in the gaslight, and the string of pearls that wound about her neck emphasized the swell of her bosom. She laughed, causing the tiny, artful curls around her face to bounce.

This might not have been the world Fontaine had been born into, but it was obvious that she belonged. Mr. Prue stood at her side, beaming at the crowd. It reminded Rosemary of a thought she'd had weeks ago, that Fontaine would have made a remarkable politician, if she were only a man. The force of her personality drew people to her, as did her empathy. But when Rosemary looked closer, a different story became apparent. Fontaine held a flute of champagne that she had not sipped from once, clutched Mr. Prue's arm in a crushing grip, and darted her gaze around the crowd every few minutes.

As reluctant as Rosemary was to leave Fontaine to the mercy of Mr. Prue and his guests, she had not suffered the awful choice of attire to stand like a wallflower all night. With Fontaine serving as a distraction, it was Rosemary's turn to search their host's office. Convincing him to release Peter and Quinn was no longer enough. They needed proof they could bring to the authorities in Halifax to have Mr. Prue arrested. Well, that was what Fontaine wanted. Rosemary was practical enough to know they stood little chance of getting anyone in Halifax to take them seriously.

Regardless, they needed leverage, and she had some idea of where she might find it. Mr. Prue now kept the door to his office locked. But she'd learned several tricks from Saffron since her niece had married. The viscountess had laughingly refused to disclose who had taught her but had convinced Rosemary of the value of such a skill after she had lost the key to her favorite jewelry box. When she reached the door, she removed two hairpins from her coiffure and knelt. It took longer than expected, and with every second that passed, she expected a footman or maid to appear and ask what she was doing.

Click.

She turned the doorknob, slipped inside, and collapsed on the ground. She had never felt so alive in her life. No wonder Saffron had embraced adventure. The heady rush of excitement had her breathless to the point of dizziness. When she no longer felt on the verge of fainting, she struggled to her feet and searched for the shape of a desk in the darkness. The curtains were drawn tight and she soon smacked her knee on a table. She limped over to the windows and pulled a curtain open so that a bright rectangle of moonlight bloomed over Mr. Prue's desk. There was no one outside to see her, but she would do her search quickly. She didn't want Mr. Prue noticing that she was missing.

She tugged open the first drawer to reveal a disorganized collection of documents, which she removed and placed on top of the desk. To her dismay, the papers didn't seem to be in any semblance of order. There were jotted notes about the staff, lists of books that Mr. Prue presumably wanted to purchase, and a sketch of two women performing a licentious act that she mentally jotted down for the future to try.

She finished the stack and returned it to the drawer in the same order. There had to be something they could use. She wouldn't leave his office empty-handed.

The sound of voices came from the hallway. She rushed over to the window and tugged the curtain back in place, then scurried beneath the desk.

"Mr. Prue is very particular about who cleans this room," Mrs. Feather said in her usual clipped tones. Some of the tightness in Rosemary's shoulders eased. Having Mrs. Feather find her sneaking about Mr. Prue's office was not nearly as bad as being caught by their host or a guest. As stern as Mrs. Feather acted, Rosemary was confident that she wasn't immune to bribery, if it came to that.

"Yes, Mrs. Feather," a second voice said, and Rosemary almost gave herself away with a laugh. It was Annie. Of course. Annie must have seen the housekeeper about to enter Mr. Prue's room and involved herself to avoid Rosemary being caught.

Rosemary peered through a slit in the desk as Mrs. Feather lit several candles, then briskly showed Annie the cleaning that Mr. Prue expected. As they approached her hiding space, the dizziness that had struck Rosemary earlier returned. She tensed all of her muscles and closed her eyes, waiting for a gasp or scream or some other sign that she'd been found.

Instead, Mrs. Feather stopped on the other side of the desk. "And we do not touch Mr. Prue's desk. Not even to dust. Do you understand that, girl?"

"Yes," Annie said meekly. "May I clean now, Mrs. Feather?"

The housekeeper mumbled something. Then there was the creak of the door opening and closing, followed by a giggle.

Rosemary rose from her spot to find Annie dutifully dusting the shelves of Mr. Prue's bookcase.

"I accidentally dropped a stack of plates," Annie said. "Mrs. Feather's punishment was to make me clean this room. Most of the servants refuse to come in here. Mr. Prue has a rather bad habit of sacking anyone who moves even a single item out of place." She thwacked her feather duster against the spines of the books that were carefully arranged on the shelves, scattering dust everywhere. "I guess Mrs. Feather didn't train me that well."

Rosemary winced. "One shouldn't take one's anger out on inanimate objects, Annie."

The girl dropped the duster. "Fine. What're you looking for, then? Can I help? Being a maid is boring."

"You can help by locking the door."

As the girl did as she'd been told, Rosemary returned to her searching. She checked another drawer and dug through the contents until she'd reached an indent in the bottom that felt out of place.

"What is it?" Annie asked, from over Rosemary's shoulder. "Did you find something?"

"I'm not sure," Rosemary said. "I think there might…" She reached deeper into the drawer until her fingertips touched something smooth. "There it is." She withdrew her arm, pulled out the upper drawer, and held it above her head. A thin book bound in red leather was slotted into a clever groove. She removed the book and opened it at random.

Annie took one look at the thin, slanted writing and scowled.

"Scribbles."

"Not quite," Rosemary said. She flipped a page and read the first two rows aloud. "'*Gilly, 14, Borrington factory, fifty cents a week. Mark, 12, Gradero mine, three dollars a week.*'"

"Names, ages, where he's sent them, and how much he's getting for their work," Annie said. She tapped her finger on the opposite page. "But what's these marks, then?"

As Rosemary looked at the cross-hatched lines Annie had pointed to, a shiver went down her back. She couldn't be certain, but it looked as if Mr. Prue had not only kept a meticulous record of every child he had leased, but also the ones who had died.

A shout came from the hallway. Rosemary shoved the small book into her pocket. It wasn't definitive proof, but it would have to be enough, as they had run out of time.

They rushed toward the door, only to have it open in front of them. Mr. Prue blocked their path with a key in his hand and a wicked smile on his face.

She felt as if a bucket of ice-cold water had been dropped over her.

"What a coincidence, Mrs. Summersby," he said. "I was just looking for you." He turned his head toward Annie and raised his eyebrows. "What is your name, girl?"

Annie ducked her head. "Margaret, sir. I wasn't helping Mrs. Summersby, sir, I swear. I was just doing the cleaning Mrs. Feather assigned."

Mr. Prue clucked his tongue. "Another clever liar. Lady Kerry must be quite fond of you. What good fortune catching you both at the same time."

Annie took a step away from Rosemary. "Not a liar, sir. My mom always said I had a good heart and was never to be lying to my employers." She kept moving, and Rosemary realized with a start that Annie was forcing Mr. Prue to choose. With no other servants to assist him—the hallway behind him was empty—he couldn't corner both of them.

"Stop moving, girl," Mr. Prue said. He jerked his head back

and forth between Annie and Rosemary. Soon, he would decide which of them he wanted more, and the odds were good it wouldn't be Annie.

Rosemary's throat tightened. She could either leave Annie, who seemed determined to handle Mr. Prue on her own, or become involved and risk both of them being captured. Would Fontaine be angry with her if she abandoned Annie to save herself?

Of course she would. It was exactly the opposite of what Fontaine would've done.

That realization made her decision much easier.

She brought her heel down on Mr. Prue's foot. Even with his sturdy boots, he howled and fell to the floor. Rosemary grabbed Annie's hand and ran.

"Which way do we go?" Annie asked as they turned down a servants' hallway. "The front entrance, or the rear?"

"Neither," Rosemary said. "We aren't leaving without the others."

As irrational as it was to risk their freedom, and as much as Fontaine would have told them to escape without her, Rosemary understood now why Fontaine had been unable to leave the sickly Quinn in the workhouse. It wasn't just that Rosemary had formed an emotional connection to each member of their small group, but she knew that her heart would grow cold if she allowed rationality to make every choice for her. She never wanted to return to being the kind of person who scoffed at the idea of supporting a charity for reasons other than being fashionable and had looked the other way when Mr. Blake had assaulted Lady Mason. Neither would she commit herself to the wellbeing of others as wholly as Fontaine did, to the point of self-sacrifice. She would always be the benefactor to the baroness, helping Fontaine achieve her goals in any way possible.

Annie grinned. "I was hoping you would say that. I know where Mr. Prue stashed Quinn and Peter. Follow me."

Rosemary's lungs burned with exertion, and her thighs would

be aching for days, but she kept up with Annie as the girl turned a corner to a narrow staircase and descended the steps three at a time. The sound of shouting reached them, with Mr. Prue's voice clear among them.

They went all the way to the basement, where the floors were damp stone and the foggy windows were lined with bars. The sound of many people walking above them suggested they were beneath the ballroom, but it could also have been the kitchen. In the chaos of escaping Mr. Prue, she had lost all sense of direction.

"Here," Annie said, slapping a hand on a door, which was shackled with a padlock. Rosemary started to remove her hairpins when Annie grabbed a brick from the ground and smashed it against the lock. Sparks flew as she hammered until the still-engaged padlock and the flimsy, broken shackle fell to the floor. She kicked the fragments, sending them spinning into the corner.

"Clever trick," Rosemary said.

Annie grinned. "Locks are no good without proper housing, and Mr. Prue's a cheap bastard." Then she grasped the door and heaved it open. It made a terrible sound as it scraped against the floor, but when it opened, Quinn and Peter were indeed inside. Except they weren't cowering on the soggy cots on the floor or running toward Rosemary with their arms outstretched. Peter was holding Quinn up as he squirmed between the bars of a broken window. If Quinn's rapidly disappearing legs were any sign, the boys had nearly freed themselves from the basement with no assistance.

Annie cleared her throat, and Peter spun around, raising his hands as if to fight. When he saw Rosemary, his snarling expression transformed into one of shock. He reached up and tugged his brother's foot, the only part of the boy that remained inside the room.

"Quinn didn't believe me," Peter said, scrubbing the tears from his face. "I told him Lady Kerry would never leave us down here."

Rosemary scoffed. "Only Lady Kerry?"

Peter launched himself at her. She caught his skinny body and squeezed him while Annie ran to the window.

"Thank you," Peter whispered. Then he pushed away and put his hands on his hips. "Now, what're we going to do to get back at Mr. Prue?"

"*We* aren't doing anything," she said. "You, Annie, and Oliver are going to get far away from this place." She held up a hand as he started to protest. "No excuses." Then she removed the slim, red book from her pocket and pressed it into Peter's hands. "I need you to keep this safe until I see you again. Can you do that?"

Peter clutched the book to his chest and frowned. "What about you?"

She looked out the open door to the dank hall. Water dripped from the ceiling and formed puddles on the floor, and the sound of pounding above them had increased. Mr. Prue was likely searching the house for them.

"I'm going back for Lady Kerry."

Chapter Thirty

HOW LONG HAD it been since Mr. Prue had left the ballroom? A buzzing filled Fontaine, making it difficult for her to stand still. She circled the room once before turning on her heel and dashing toward the exit. It was as she'd feared. There were no servants anywhere. Something had to have gone wrong.

Her suspicions were confirmed when she reached the kitchen to find Mrs. Feather and other servants shouting about a thief. She gathered her voluminous skirts in her hands and ran for the stairs, only to crash into Rosemary.

"There you are," she said, grasping Fontaine's upper arms. "That's good luck. I was coming to find you."

"You're okay," Fontaine whispered. Then she threw her arms around the other woman, closed her eyes tightly and inhaled the fresh, floral smell of Rosemary's hair. She had never felt so safe as she did at that moment, tucked securely in Rosemary's embrace.

She pulled back and pressed her lips to Rosemary's in a searing kiss. When Rosemary returned the passion in equal measure, delving her tongue into Fontaine's mouth and grasping at her clothes, logic reasserted itself. Fontaine pulled back and pressed a final kiss to Rosemary's lips before putting her at arm's length.

"What happened?" she asked.

Rosemary wiped her lips with the back of her hand. "I found the proof we need. Annie, Quinn, and Peter are already out. I came back for you."

Fontaine's eyes burned. She gave Rosemary another crushing hug. "Thank you."

"That's the rule," Rosemary said. "We leave no one behind."

Tears choked Fontaine's throat, but she managed a hoarse laugh.

Then they split apart and, without having to discuss what they were going to do next, made for the rear exit of the house. With the servants in chaos, it was surprisingly easy to force their way through the narrow halls until they burst through a heavy door and into an alley.

"What now?" Fontaine asked, her breath forming a cloud in the chilly air. She wrapped her bare arms around herself. The alley continued for a block in either direction, letting out on two busy streets. "Which way?"

BOOM.

The door behind them flew open and a red-faced Mr. Prue lurched toward them, with Mrs. Feather following closely behind.

Fontaine grabbed Rosemary's hand and ran north, while wondering what, exactly, Mr. Prue intended. She couldn't imagine him physically restraining her. He seemed more the type to achieve his goals through blackmail and intimidation.

She picked up speed, and they reached the street in time to see Mr. Perkin's cab quickly approaching them, with Xavier in the driver's spot. The door opened, and Annie waved from inside.

"They were supposed to escape," Rosemary said between gasping breaths.

"Lady Kerry, wait!" Mr. Prue yelled.

Rosemary tugged her hand, but Fontaine kept her feet planted. She couldn't run from Mr. Prue forever. He had wealth and resources, not to mention influence over the businesses and factories that were benefiting from all the children that had been sent to London.

"What are you doing?" Rosemary asked. She tugged Fontaine's hand again.

"Let me talk to him," Fontaine said.

She had to try to find a diplomatic solution before they resorted to methods that had much less chance of success. Everything she had tried thus far had been rooted in the idea that she could make him understand and care about the suffering he was causing, but that was how Fontaine saw the world. Mr. Prue was foremost a businessman. She understood now that appealing to his emotions would never have worked. The tool she needed was one that Rosemary wielded so well—cold, rational logic.

"Are you sure about this?" Rosemary asked.

"I am," Fontaine said. "I didn't tell you before because I was trying to protect you, but Mr. Prue all but admitted to burning down the Halifax Home."

Rosemary gave her a look full of horror. "What?"

"He has blood on his hands. If we run, I don't think he'll ever stop chasing us." Then she linked her arm with Rosemary's and waited as Mr. Prue stomped the last few feet to stand before her, all but radiating anger. He drew himself up and attempted to look down his nose at her, a tactic that failed due to them being nearly the same height.

"I could have Mrs. Summersby arrested for theft, Lady Kerry," Mr. Prue said. "Mrs. Feather and I both saw her steal a book from my office."

Rosemary's arm stiffened. "You lie."

"It would be your word against hers," Fontaine said, taking care to keep her voice level and free of emotion. "I am sure we can come up with an alternative arrangement."

Mr. Prue narrowed his eyes. "What are you proposing?"

"That you sever all ties with the foundation and pursue other business in Halifax."

He shook his head. "My dear Lady Kerry, that is exactly what I was trying to do." He held out his hands, palms up. "It is only now that they've seen you on my arm that the wealthy members of this city pay me the respect I am due. I cannot change without you. I cannot become a *better man* without you."

Fontaine shuddered. The way his voice crooned, his slow

approach and wide eyes—all of it was clearly designed to prey on her emotions. He was trying to manipulate her, just as she had decided to manipulate him.

It wouldn't work.

"What will it take?" Mr. Prue asked. A thread of desperation had entered his voice. "I'll fund your school. I'll give you whatever you want."

He stepped closer. "You could remain with your companion during my frequent travels. I would stay away from you as much as possible." He gently took her hands and lowered his voice. "Think of all the good you could do."

In her entire life, her brain and her heart had never been more at odds. She could imagine the life Mr. Prue described easily. Halifax society would accept her as the wife of a prominent businessman. She would be free to find sponsors for any of her charitable initiatives. Then each night she could return to Rosemary's arms.

Her thoughts jerked to a halt.

Rosemary.

What right did Fontaine have to dictate the course of their lives? This decision would impact Rosemary as much as her. Perhaps more, as Rosemary had family waiting for her in London.

"Give me a moment," Fontaine said. Then she turned around, walked a few steps, and faced Rosemary. "What do you think? We could stay here. Together."

Rosemary's lips opened. Closed. Opened again. She sighed. "You should do it."

The resignation in her voice made something tight inside Fontaine's chest unwind and told her everything she needed to know. Keeping their relationship a secret was necessary, but she didn't want to live with a husband. Every night she spent at Mr. Prue's side would feel like a betrayal. She squared her shoulders and returned to Mr. Prue.

As if sensing he'd failed, he scowled. "Are you really willing to abandon the children you sent here? I don't think you can. If you leave, knowing that I am in control, you'll never be able to forgive yourself. I could have them placed in far more dangerous conditions. Perhaps the mines. By the time you return, there won't be any of them left. What's more, you might find your reception in London is not what you expect."

The way he said those words made Fontaine erupt into gooseflesh. "What have you done?"

His smile was wicked. "You are familiar with Mr. Blake, I believe? He was here recently to do a few things for his employer."

"I knew I saw him on the ship," Rosemary whispered.

Mr. Prue waved his hand in the air. "Mr. Blake told me about what happened at the Whitechapel workhouse. That's how I learned what you were doing, *Frannie*. As you had become a problem and I desired a titled wife, encouraging you to travel here was an ideal solution for us both."

The way he spoke of her, like a pawn in a game of chess to be moved at his leisure, made Fontaine want to strike him, but there were too many questions unanswered.

"Before Mr. Blake left, I gave him a letter," Mr. Prue continued. "In it, I described your *particular* preferences. My own manner of insurance."

"You know?" Fontaine reached out and grabbed his upper arms. "How?"

Mr. Prue shrugged out of her grip. "The way you spoke of Mrs. Summersby made it obvious that she meant more to you than a mere *companion*. Not to mention the fidgety, defensive way Mrs. Summersby acted around you. But you do not need to worry. I instructed Mr. Blake not to open the letter unless he learns that we have not married or that I am in trouble."

"That's enough," Rosemary said. She tugged Fontaine's arm, pulling her back until they were several feet away from Mr. Prue. That was perhaps for the best, as Fontaine had imagined strangling the man for the briefest of moments.

"So, you see, you are better off remaining with me," Mr. Prue said.

"I'm sorry, Mr. Prue, but you are mistaken," Fontaine said, although her voice shook with tears. "Do what you will, but I will not marry you."

Mr. Prue's smile faltered. "You cannot leave. You—You—" Twin spots of red appeared on his cheeks. "Be sensible, woman! You cannot expect to achieve anything with"—he waved his arm, encompassing Fontaine and the nearby coach—"this group. How are you even going to get back? I have connections in this city. You'll never find a captain willing to transport you."

"Don't be so sure about that," Rosemary said. Then she raised her hand in a wave.

Fontaine spun, her heart in her throat. Cookie and Winter were making their way down the street toward them, with Captain Charles following behind.

"I was told you might be in need of assistance," Captain Charles said, when he reached them. "I would be honored to transport you to London."

"No!" Mr. Prue cried. He grabbed for her, but Captain Charles stepped neatly between them and grasped Mr. Prue's upper arm. "There will be none of that, sir. You will not assault ladies while I am here to stop you."

Then James appeared behind Captain Charles, a vicious scowl on his face. "I've got a few friends who've lost 'prentices and would like to have a word with this one, if you don't mind, cap'n."

The sheer look of terror on Mr. Prue's face as Captain Charles handed him over to James replayed in Fontaine's mind for days to come.

Chapter Thirty-One

As Fontaine leaned on the railing of Captain Charles's steamship, a crowd of tradesmen and dock workers gathered around Mr. Prue, who had been dragged out of the city by James and Cookie.

"What's going to happen to him?" Annie asked.

Fontaine didn't know how to answer. It felt as if there were a splinter slowly digging itself deeper into her chest, making it difficult for her to breathe. She couldn't think about the children she was leaving behind without feeling nauseated. Instead of rescuing them herself, she had to trust James and the others to work in her stead. It wasn't what the Fontaine of even a month ago would have done, but Rosemary had shown her that doing everything herself was impossible.

A seagull screamed overhead, and a spray of mist hit Fontaine in the face, making her wince.

"He'll face justice eventually," Rosemary said, joining them at the railing. "There's nothing more we can do."

Rosemary was right, of course, but that didn't stop her from feeling that splinter sink deeper into her heart. She smoothed her hand over her pocket, which contained the book Rosemary had stolen. Between what they'd seen, the letters she'd taken from Mr. Prue's desk, and the notebook, she had to hope it would be enough to convince the board to expel Mr. Blake.

The people on the shore had grown so small that she could

barely see them. Despite that, she could still feel the stares, as if all the children she had left behind were standing near the water. So many had already died and would continue to suffer while she sailed back to London. If only she could have communicated with the board some other way, but she didn't trust that any other communication would not be misinterpreted or diverted. Only a face-to-face interaction would do.

"I asked the captain to assign us the same cabin we had before," Rosemary said. "I didn't think you'd mind."

Fontaine sniffed. "Thank you."

Rosemary chuckled. "For what? For interrupting your impending marriage, or for ensuring we'll have privacy on the return trip to London?"

Fontaine chuckled. "All of it, and more."

She tilted her head onto Rosemary's shoulder and closed her eyes. "I couldn't have done any of this without you."

Rosemary snorted. "Sure, you could have, but you would have given away all of your possessions and would have ended up married to Mr. Prue."

Fontaine giggled again. Rosemary was right. She had been so consumed with guilt because she hadn't felt she deserved anything in her life. Including Rosemary's affection.

But she'd been wrong.

It didn't matter the circumstances. What had happened in Halifax was not her fault, and the only person who owed the relocated orphans was Mr. Prue. There was only so much one woman could do. She couldn't be in two places at once, and although she knew she had to fight to get more people to help her, not take it all on her shoulders, marrying a man was out of the question. What she and Rosemary had was special, and Fontaine would not sacrifice it, or herself, for anything.

"We won't be able to keep doing this when we return," Fontaine whispered. "Not if Mr. Prue's letter arrives before us." Without the protection of a husband, she would have to be completely respectable to survive the inevitable scandal. That meant distancing herself from Rosemary.

"London is days away," Rosemary whispered. "This time that we have is ours until then."

"What should we do with that time?" Fontaine asked. She slid her hand down Rosemary's back.

What she needed was a distraction. The more she thought about the board, the more anxious she got. Better to put it out of her mind. At least for a while.

Rosemary turned in Fontaine's embrace, and their lips came together with no hesitation.

"Bunk," Rosemary whispered against her mouth.

They made it to the privacy of their room in record time. Then Fontaine was clawing at her gown with a fervor, tugging laces and yanking each layer off of her until she wore only her underthings. Rosemary remained fully clothed as she pushed Fontaine onto their bunk.

"Watch me."

Rosemary lifted her arms to her hair and pulled the pins out, one by one, to clatter onto the floor. Each lock of hair that fell stoked the embers burning inside Fontaine. She wanted to reach out, but as she crawled closer, Rosemary crossed her arms.

"Touch yourself," she said.

Fontaine flushed. *"That's* what you want?"

Rosemary grinned. "I want to watch you pleasure yourself while you watch me."

She gulped and removed her shift, leaving her bare aside from her stockings, then spread her legs and brought her fingers to her sex. She was already dripping wet and ready. As she massaged herself, Rosemary shed layers one at a time while swishing her lips and fluttering her eyes. When she was down to her shift, Fontaine licked her lips. The dusky shape of Rosemary's nipples was visible through the thin linen.

She imagined those breasts pressed to her mouth and worked herself with an increasing fervor. As she sped up, so did Rosemary. She lifted her shift over her head, revealing every inch of delicious skin, and the triangle of curls at the apex of her thighs. She spun around, circling her hips, bearing the smooth skin of her buttocks and the curve of her back.

Fontaine wasn't sure which view she preferred more.

Rosemary spun back around and crouched forward, stretching her arms toward Fontaine's ankles. The prickling of nails on her skin sent electric tingles up her body, and she had to resist the urge to curl her legs to her chest.

Having Rosemary between her legs was exactly where she wanted her.

"Don't stop," Rosemary whispered as she began kissing up from Fontaine's ankle. "I want to see you finish. I want to feel you tremble as pleasure courses through you. Then I want to taste you as you shiver with desire."

Fontaine panted as she worked herself, growing wetter by the moment. She imagined Rosemary bringing her lips to join Fontaine's hands, felt the phantom kisses and plunge of a tongue inside her.

A fluttering began in her stomach, but she wasn't quite ready to orgasm. She slowed her movements, eliciting a glance from Rosemary.

"So that is your trick," Rosemary said. "Well, I rather think I can beat you at that one." She put her hands on Fontaine's thighs and spread them apart in a smooth motion that made her feel as if she were being opened for inspection. Then Rosemary brought her lips down and began movements that quickly brought Fontaine back to the edge. She clutched at the sheets, wanting yet more pleasure.

"You're very good," Rosemary said. Then she pressed the tips of two fingers slowly into Fontaine and curled them upward. The pressure and sensation were too much. The orgasm rippled through her body, making her cry out until she collapsed in a boneless heap. Her skin was covered in sweat, and she felt raw inside, but in a good way.

Rosemary shifted to lie atop her, one knee draped over Fontaine's legs, her head on Fontaine's chest.

"What about you?" Fontaine asked as she brought her arm around Rosemary. She trailed her fingertips along the soft skin of Rosemary's back, then tangled them in her hair.

"Not yet," Rosemary said. "I want to enjoy the feeling of you spent beneath me first. I never want to forget what this feels like."

The sadness in her voice had Fontaine turned so they were facing each other. "I'm sorry for doubting you. You were right about everything, but I was too stubborn to see it. Sacrificing myself would have accomplished nothing. It would have just made me miserable."

Rosemary brushed the backs of her fingers against Fontaine's cheek. "I was stubborn, too. Selfish. I wanted you all to myself. I didn't want to think about the consequences or about so many children being harmed. It used to be easy not to think about anyone else."

Fontaine sniffed. "Mr. Prue was right about one thing. It would give us a way out if I married a man. The committee would be more willing to dismiss Mr. Prue's claims, even if they had already received his letter. Depending on which man I chose, I might even have sway over politics."

Rosemary tensed. "You could."

Fontaine squeezed her arms around Rosemary. "But I won't because I can't imagine living without you. I don't want to spend another night without you."

Rosemary squeezed her back. "You are too sentimental." Her words were terse, but there was a waver in her voice.

"Let's make a deal," Fontaine said, coming up on her elbow so she could look down into Rosemary's face. "We won't give up hope until we arrive." She touched Rosemary's cheek. "I want to enjoy every moment I have with you before the rest of the world intrudes."

A tear slid down from Rosemary's eye toward her ear. Fontaine caught it and wiped it away, then kissed the spot where it had trailed. Then she kissed lower until Rosemary was squirming beneath her.

True to their promise, Rosemary didn't speak of their future again that night because Fontaine ensured that every sound that came out of her mouth was an inarticulate cry.

Chapter Thirty-Two

THE DAYS PASSED in a blissful haze. Fontaine occupied her time reading the few books she could find or making herself useful by mending tears in clothing or entertaining the first-class guests by playing the pianoforte. Rosemary joined her in most of these tasks, sitting beside her as they chatted about everyday matters, avoiding all discussion of what would happen at the end of the journey. With each sunrise, an increasing sense of desperation filled her, even as she tried not to think about what awaited them.

The nights, though.

The nights were different.

Fontaine went to her cabin every evening, eager to explore more of Rosemary's body. She never tired of finding new ways to make Rosemary gasp. Through their explorations, they discovered a strip of highly sensitive skin along Fontaine's spine, and a similar spot on Rosemary's thigh. No matter how tired they were at the end of each day, they spared at least an hour to enjoy themselves. This time proved increasingly necessary for Fontaine, as their activities allowed her to shed the mounting anxiety she felt with the passing of time.

It was on the last day of their journey, according to the captain, that Fontaine finally allowed herself to consider what would happen when they arrived in London. She was lying beside Rosemary on a hammock they had strung up inside their cabin, staring at the even planks of the ceiling, feeling the gentle motion of the ship rocking back and forth, when she said, "Would you marry me?"

Rosemary made a choking sound. "W-What? Two women cannot marry. Not in London or Halifax."

She pursed her lips. "I know. But what if we could? Would you marry me?"

Rosemary rolled on her side and put her head on Fontaine's chest, a position they had found was one of the most comfortable for both of them in the swinging mesh hammock. "Of course I would. Why do you ask?"

She wasn't entirely sure. The idea had popped into her mind, the way so many things had when she had been a child and had dreamed of attracting the attention of a wealthy family. She had spent hours as a child imagining what it would be like to go to sleep without feeling the pangs of hunger, to wear clothes that were not grimy and full of holes. Perhaps that was why, when she'd achieved those moments, it hadn't felt real. If she had imagined them, how could they possibly have come true?

"Is it time to discuss what will happen tomorrow?" Rosemary asked.

"I think it is." She stared at a crack in the floor above her that bisected a plank, dividing it into two ragged sections of roughly equal size. "If Mr. Blake reads that letter before we arrive and learns of our relationship, he will tell the board, and they will expel me." This was something they both had known for weeks, but she had to get the words out of her mind. Denying Mr. Prue's claims would be painful, but she would do it if it meant they could stay together. The problem was that it would only work if the board had not already turned against her. They didn't know if Mr. Blake had opened the letter from Mr. Prue and spread the news. They might be returning to London to discover their names in every newspaper in the city.

"There is still a chance, however small," Rosemary said. She traced a circle with her finger on Fontaine's chest. "Don't give up yet."

Fontaine hated Mr. Prue and Mr. Blake for ruining her chance at having everything she wanted. If it weren't for their spiteful act, they could have continued their relationship in secret. Women living with companions was common. Two widowed women cohabiting would hardly be glanced at twice. It was not as if either of them were debutantes.

But the odds of them arriving before Mr. Blake opened Mr. Prue's letter were slim. The moment Mr. Blake learned of her predilection, he would tell everyone he knew. Within days, she would no longer receive the invitations she relied upon to charm members of the *ton* into supporting her causes.

There had to be a way for her to gather benefactors without participating in the balls and other events that members of the *ton* were so fond of. She had never enjoyed flaunting her wealth or speaking words she didn't mean. If she had to give up society, she would gladly do so if she could find a replacement source of funding.

If only they had another source of wealth. Then they could be happy together without requiring the help of patrons.

There had to be a way. They just had to find it.

Chapter Thirty-Three

ROSEMARY SHOULD HAVE been relieved when she spotted land on the horizon. The charade was almost over. Their only remaining hope was that Mr. Blake had not opened Mr. Prue's letter already, although they both thought that unlikely. When he realized that Fontaine was not going to marry Mr. Prue, he would tell everyone their secret.

She tilted her weight as the ship rocked. After so many days at sea, it was no longer difficult. She had even begun predicting when the swells would come, tensing her body and finding a place to anchor herself before she went sprawling.

Unfortunately, she was not so lucky when it came to Fontaine. She never knew what the dowager baroness would say next. It had been frustrating at first, but she had grown used to the change in routine. Now she craved Fontaine by her side.

"Rough waters," Captain Charles said, coming to stand beside her.

"How long before we arrive?" Rosemary asked. She hoped he would say that they couldn't approach the docks because of the weather. Then she would have more time.

"Less than an hour," the captain said.

Rosemary deflated like a pricked balloon. "I see."

She had to push her feelings aside. Fontaine had an important task, informing the committee of what they had seen. The longer they delayed, the more children might be harmed in the positions they had been forced into. Even if it meant Fontaine was giving up some of what she loved, a part of herself, Rosemary had to step away and let Fontaine deal with Mr. Blake. If she denied the accusations and had no further contact with Rosemary, she might still save her position. It was not just about them, but all the children of Halifax and London. Their lives were worth more than both Rosemary and Fontaine's happiness.

If only they could have both. But Mr. Prue had likely already ruined their chance of being able to pretend to be widowed companions.

"I met a young lady once, many years ago," the captain said. "I've never known a more vivacious woman. Every sailor aboard my ship respected her. I had thoughts of asking her to be my wife."

Rosemary glanced up at the man. He was bent over the railing with his elbows on the wood and his eyes had taken on a faraway look. She recognized that look as one Fontaine wore often. It meant she was remembering something from her past.

"Why didn't you?" she asked.

The captain scratched his beard. "I was afraid."

She scoffed. "You? Afraid?" This coming from the man who had stood up to Mr. Prue.

The captain shrugged. "Not for me, Mrs. Summersby. I was afraid that if I latched her to this life, my love would not be enough to sustain her. She was a fiery ball of ambition. She wanted to be a captain of her own right. As no one would hire her, her only option was to become a pirate. I could not deny her that, even if the danger was worrisome. But then again, that's what I loved about her. Her reckless independence. Her fierce spirit. So, instead of asking her to join me, I let her go." He frowned. "With every day that passes, I regret not following her."

Something warm curled in her stomach. "Even though you have your ship and your men?"

The captain closed his eyes. "The life I have here is the only one I have ever known, but that doesn't mean I have to be trapped by it. My men would have found a new captain, but I do not believe I will ever find anyone who sparks my fire more than Yelena." He glanced at her. "Sometimes the choice that seems the most difficult is the one we must take."

"A difficult *legal* path is not the same as one that is illegal," she said, although she understood what he meant. He implied she feared changing Fontaine. It was true. She didn't want to crush Fontaine's dreams. If they stayed together, Mr. Blake would reveal their relationship to the board, if not the whole of society. They would become social outcasts. Everything Fontaine had worked so hard for would come crumbling down.

"I...I cannot be what she needs," she said. "The only way she can save herself is by keeping her distance from me."

Or marrying a man, she thought, although she couldn't quite say those words aloud.

The captain's eyes gleamed. "Are you sure of that?"

She stared at him. "What do you mean?"

The captain pushed back from the railing. "I think perhaps you are not considering what Lady Kerry needs."

She snorted. "What could she need that I could give her? I live on the fringes of my niece's land. I have no title, no fortune. The invitations I receive are out of politeness or because the person inviting me wishes some boon." She turned back to the sea and the rapidly approaching shore. "There's nothing I can give her she doesn't have already."

"If that's what you believe, then perhaps you are right," the captain said. Then he turned, and the sound of his boots on the deck retreated, leaving her to stand at the bow of the ship alone, dreading what was coming.

Still, the captain's words swirled in her mind. There was a deeper meaning there. If she could only grasp it, she might figure out something important about herself and her situation. But every time she had it, it flitted out of her reach, like trying to catch a wisp of smoke.

She frowned at the horizon. There were plenty of ships, of

course, but there were also far more people than she had expected at such an early hour. As the ship came closer, she recognized some of the figures waiting by the shore.

A knot of tension in Rosemary's stomach tightened and several long minutes later, her heart leaped in her throat. The crowd included Saffron and Leo. Angelica and her husband, Simon Mayweather. Even the Marquess of Lowell and Olivia.

She clutched at the railing as a wave of dizziness passed over her. Almost everyone she cared about was waiting for her, as if they had known she was arriving. But how was that possible? She had barely had time to pen a letter to her nieces before they had left. She hadn't sent a telegram or any other notice.

"Ah, they received my message," Fontaine said.

Rosemary spun. Fontaine stood in the middle of the deck with a grin spread across her face.

"'Your message'?" Rosemary repeated.

Fontaine strode forward and put her hands on the railing. "I asked the captain if I could use his telegram to notify your friends and family that you were returning." She grinned. "I thought, after being away from them for so long, that you might be happy to have a greeting party."

Rosemary blinked several times to keep tears from falling down her cheeks but ultimately failed. She threw her arms around Fontaine, careful not to do anything more that might be visible from the shore and whispered in Fontaine's ear, "Thank you."

Fontaine squeezed her tightly for a moment, then pushed away and gave her a brittle smile. "I told you there were people waiting for you."

"But not for you."

Fontaine had made her family in the children she rescued.

But what if she had a family to ask for help?

The seed of an idea worked its way into the fertile soil of her mind. Before it could sprout roots, the ship shuddered, and they were swept away from the railing. The next few moments were filled with shouting and chaos on the deck. Rosemary pulled Fontaine out of the way, and they pressed themselves to the bow of the ship. They should probably have returned to their bunk, but it was too exciting watching everything happen, and she worried that if she stopped looking at Saffron on the shore, her niece would vanish.

Finally, the gangplank was set down, and she hurried off the boat. Angelica and Saffron rushed to her and threw their arms about her, tears running down their faces, as if she had been gone for months or years and not simply weeks.

"We thought you would never come back," Saffron said. "You must never do that again!"

Rosemary looked back and forth between Angelica and Saffron in confusion. "It was only a few weeks."

Then, as she watched Saffron's lower lip tremble, it hit her. She had done exactly what Basil had done: departed London on a ship with only a letter to tell her family where she'd gone.

Before she had left, she might have brushed off such concerns as being overly emotional. She wouldn't have stopped to consider Saffron's feelings. She likely wouldn't have connected anything Saffron had said or done to Basil. But after everything that had happened during her journey, she finally understood how her niece felt.

"I'm so sorry," she said. "I never…I shouldn't have left without speaking to you. It was wrong of me. I tried to write, but it was harder than expected."

Saffron's jaw dropped. "You did?" She shook her head. "You have to tell me everything that has happened. I think we've missed quite a lot."

Chapter Thirty-Four

Three days later

FONTAINE STOOD IN front of a long table in the main building of the foundation that had once felt like the center of her life. The members of the board who sat across from her looked both older and more tired than they had less than a month before. Even Mr. Blake, who had once attacked her in an alley, no longer seemed as intimidating. He glowered at her from his place at Mr. Hill's side, a configuration that did not bode well for Fontaine's case.

She wondered whom he had told about the contents of Mr. Prue's letter and why he had not yet raised the subject of her relationship with Rosemary. Such an accusation would be sure to shift the sentiment of many of the members of the board against her. Perhaps they had gotten tremendously lucky, and he had not yet opened the letter.

Mrs. Eris shuffled a stack of papers in front of her, then cleared her throat. Every head in the room turned toward the older woman.

"Lady Kerry, I must agree that the allegations you've present-ed are quite disturbing," Mrs. Eris said. "But we cannot make such an important decision so quickly, especially not without a proper investigation."

Fontaine's spirits sank. She'd feared that the careful Mrs. Eris would say just that and would encourage the board to put together a sub-committee to look into her claims. The formation of that group would take weeks, or even months. She didn't have time to wait for bureaucracy.

That left only one option.

"I call for a vote of no confidence," Fontaine said.

Mrs. Eris clutched her blouse.

Mr. Blake gave her a look so full of malice, she was surprised he didn't leap across the table and throttle her.

"A vote of what now?" Mr. Hill asked.

"I am calling your leadership into question," she said, pitching her voice loud enough that even the elderly Mr. Hill could not mistake her intent.

"Nonsense," Mr. Hill sputtered. "You do not have the right."

Mrs. Eris cleared her throat. "I'm afraid she does. She is a full member of the board. On what grounds do you raise this motion, Lady Kerry?"

The sweat dripping down Mr. Hill's face made Fontaine realize something important that she couldn't believe she'd missed. Mr. Blake hadn't acted alone. That meant she had one last card to play, although it would require her to bluff.

"On the grounds that Mr. Hill knew about the situation in Halifax but said nothing." When the members of the board gasped and began muttering, she raised her voice again. "Mr. Hill, did you not have Mr. Blake correspond with Mr. Prue?"

This was it. Either the board would support her, or they would dismiss her from their ranks, and she would likely never find another position in a charitable foundation again.

Mr. Hill paled and darted his gaze about the room. "I most certainly did not." She removed the red, leatherbound notebook from her pocket and a ribbon-wrapped bundle of letters and placed them on the table. "These letters prove that Mr. Hill accepted money from Mr. Blake on behalf of Mr. Prue. I am also willing to guess that the funds did not end up in the foundation's accounts."

As far as she knew, the letters said nothing of the sort, but she hoped he would incriminate himself before anyone checked.

He tugged at his cravat. "Well, regardless of what I might or might not have done, there is no need for such a vote. I have decided to retire. Effective immediately. We can proceed with a vote for new leadership."

A murmur rippled through the room.

"As everyone knows, I support Mr. Blake," Mr. Hill said. He gestured toward his cousin. "He has demonstrated all the capabilities we're looking for in a leader, including faithfully establishing relationships with several workhouses that—"

"Derive their value from the manipulation of children," Fontaine shouted.

Several of the men around the table gaped.

"I say, Lady Kerry," Mr. Hill said. "It was not your turn to speak. Your allegations will be dealt with at the proper time."

Mrs. Eris cleared her throat. "I disagree. If we are to vote now, then I believe it is best that Lady Kerry speak, as what she has to say might impact my decision." She stretched out a wrinkled hand and grabbed the notebook just as Mr. Hill tried to snag it. She flipped it open and tilted her reading spectacles onto her nose. After less than a minute, her frown deepened. She turned a page and then set the notebook on the table with her hand atop it. "Mr. Blake, what did you do with the funds you received from the Halifax branch? Did you supply them to Mr. Hill?"

"Funds!" Mr. Blake shouted, shoving to his feet. "If we are going to speak of funds, perhaps we should also discuss Lady Kerry's *companion*."

Fontaine felt as if the ground had dropped out from under her. "Pardon?"

Mr. Blake crossed his arms, sporting a disgustingly self-satisfied smile. "If you are going to accuse me of using funds for my own benefit, then it seems only fair that your own transgressions be revealed." He turned to Mrs. Eris. "The funds the foundation provided for Lady Kerry for the past six months have not been used as a salary for a companion but deposited into her own accounts."

Mrs. Eris furrowed her brow. "Lady Kerry, is there any truth to this claim?"

Lying would have been so much easier than telling the truth. But then she would have been as bad as Mr. Hill and Mr. Blake. So even as her stomach gurgled and her head swam, she nodded. "I'm afraid it's true. However," she said, as the room erupted into chatter, "I did not use the funds for my benefit, but to pay workhouses. Not a shilling of the money the foundation paid me stayed in my accounts. I used all of it to send children to Halifax. Children the foundation has chosen not to support, through no fault of the children's own."

Mr. Hill cleared his throat. "Well, I believe we should also explore the impropriety of Lady Kerry's relationship with her companion."

Oh, no.

Fontaine stiffened as the room filled with murmurs.

Mr. Blake met Fontaine's gaze as he reached into his coat and withdrew a letter.

Her plan was quickly falling to pieces. She had to find a way to discredit Mr. Blake before he could reveal her secret. She forced her attention away from Mr. Blake and glared at Mr. Hill.

"*You* were the one who insisted I hire a companion."

Mr. Hill huffed. "Yes, but I never imagined what sort of unladylike, uncivil behaviors you two would get up to—"

"Do you mean rescuing orphans on the brink of death? Breaking into workhouses in the cover of night? All while all of you"— she waved her arm, encompassing the rest of the board—"set increasingly strict requirements about who is worthy of our assistance and act as if children are nothing more than numbers on a page?"

Several members of the board gasped.

Mrs. Eris studied the papers in front of her while smiling

widely.

"You call *me* improper?" Fontaine asked, raising her voice. "You, who defile this foundation by making deals with a man who sends children to their deaths in mines? You, who accept money stained with the blood of those we are meant to help?"

"Now, see here," Mr. Blake said. "That is not what we mean, and you know it." He brandished the letter. "Mr. Prue—"

"Is a murderer," Fontaine said. "And if that letter is written by him, anything in it cannot be trusted."

Mr. Blake's jaw dropped open. Mr. Hill's face was pale, his eyes bulging out of their sockets.

"I quite agree," Mrs. Eris said. She pushed to her feet and snatched the letter from Mr. Blake's hand.

"Well!" Mr. Hill pushed back from his chair. "I see my wishes will not be respected. I will take my leave. This is not a committee to which I will pay any further patronage."

Several other men, including Mr. Blake, rose and followed him out the door. It was a crushing blow, more so because Fontaine knew she could not continue their efforts without them.

"Quite a coup," Mrs. Eris said. "But there are still enough of us. We can form a functioning board. As to that, I support Lady Kerry's candidacy as successor to Mr. Hill."

Fontaine gaped. After what Mr. Blake had revealed, Mrs. Eris was the last person she had expected to be her sponsor.

"All in favor of the election of Lady Kerry as chair?" Mrs. Eris asked.

Two-thirds of the room raised their hands.

Fontaine blinked rapidly, too filled with gratitude to speak. The best she'd hoped for that morning was that the board would expel Mr. Hill and Mr. Blake. Now she was surrounded by men and women willing to support her.

Mrs. Eris handed the letter she had taken from Mr. Blake to Fontaine. "I believe you will want this bit of blackmail," Mrs. Eris said. "I haven't read it, of course. I agree. Let us pay no mind to the lolling tongues of blackguards. I'd rather see *uncivil* ladies who actually care about the children we help leading the way."

Fontaine gulped. "Thank you."

Mrs. Eris waggled her fingers in the air. "These hands are still good for something. Now, I believe it is time to figure out how the foundation is going to proceed. If you will take your place, Lady Kerry?"

Chapter Thirty-Five

Two years later
London, England

THE SOUND OF the chalk sliding against the blackboard, the smell of dust floating in the air, the weight of the practice book in her hand. All of it had become intimately familiar to Rosemary, such that she could no longer understand why she had been so resistant to a change in lifestyle. Surely this, educating the next generation, was far better than moping around her cottage for days at a time.

She finished a line of practice problems and turned to her students, who were dutifully scratching away with their pens on parchment. Peter and Quinn sat at the back of the room with their desks together. As she watched, Peter leaned toward his brother and whispered something in his ear. Quinn nodded, then jotted something on Peter's parchment. As if sensing her attention, Quinn looked up. When he met her gaze, he flushed and nudged his brother in the ribs with his elbow. Peter rolled his eyes and scooted his chair further away from his brother.

From any of her other pupils, she might not have allowed such behavior, but the few times she'd attempted to separate them after their return from Halifax six months prior had resulted in both behaving far more disruptively. Even the other students had noticed and had asked that she make an exception.

That was another way in which the school was different— their pupils were far better behaved. *These* children knew what a life of poverty was like, and what awaited them if they did not complete their education, although Fontaine had mentioned that Mr. and Mrs. Martin, who had helped clean up the mess Mr. Prue had left behind in Halifax, were also considering moving back to London and enrolling their children. But for now, there were no students here who had been raised by wealthy parents. Most of them were experiencing school for the first time and were still in awe of the situation in which they had found themselves, perhaps even praying each night that they would not wake to find it had all been a dream.

She returned to her seat behind her desk and flipped through her instructional booklet, a project she had started at the end of the first year of teaching. So many of the teachers they'd hired had approached schooling with the cold impatience that was often the hallmark of education, which she had once seen as superior.

She no longer believed that.

If she was occasionally stern, she made certain that her students saw that side of her as often as they saw her kindness.

She flipped a page, her attention wandering to a sealed envelope on her desk. It was personal correspondence, which was why she had resolved to wait until later to open it. But after reading the same paragraph three times, she closed her booklet with a sigh and picked up the envelope, the latest from Halifax. True to his word, James had allowed Xavier to send weekly letters. Most of them went to Fontaine, but every so often, one was addressed to her. She used a letter opener on her desk to crack the wax seal, but what lay inside wasn't a letter, but a newspaper clipping.

NEW DETAILS IN CRIMINAL OPERATION REVEALED

January 17th, 1868

Authorities have revealed shocking new details regarding a criminal operation in Halifax. Of note, sources report that a local businessman, Mr. Jonathan Prue, has been apprehended on charges of forced labor and taxation fraud. Sources also report that several children recently removed from illegal employment in gold mines are currently receiving much-needed medical attention at St. Joseph's.

Rosemary returned the clipping to the envelope with a smile as the door to the classroom opened and Fontaine peeked inside.

"Continue working," Rosemary said as a few students dropped their pens and looked up.

She joined Fontaine at the door. The dowager-baroness-turned-headmistress was dressed in a light-blue gown with full sleeves and wore her hair pulled tightly back. Every inch the professional, respectable lady. If she was bothered that they weren't invited to some events because of the disgraced Mr. Hill's and Mr. Blake's incessant rumor-spreading, Fontaine did not show it. Neither did she seem to care that those same members of the *ton* did not send their children to her school.

The London Home for Orphans didn't need any more benefactors. Viscountess Briarwood, the Marchioness of Lowell, and Olivia's good friends, the Duke and Duchess of Hestia, provided all the funding that they required, supplemented by a small endowment from the foundation. The new board, painstakingly repopulated by Fontaine before she'd stepped down to run the school, had voted unanimously to approve the endowment.

"What is it?" Rosemary asked as she exited the classroom.

"I hired the additional teacher you requested," Fontaine said. Then she stepped aside, revealing Annie dressed in a black skirt and white blouse, her hair twisted and placed beneath a cap.

"Does this mean you passed?" Rosemary asked. Annie had been living with them while she'd prepared for the teacher certification exam Fontaine had created to ensure they only hired the most competent staff. The effort she had put in to fill the gaps in her education, studying by herself and with several tutors, had impressed both Rosemary and Fontaine.

Annie beamed. "I did!" Then she straightened, clasped her hands at her breast, and lifted her chin. "I mean, yes, Mrs. Summersby. I achieved the highest score in my class."

"Will she do?" Fontaine asked, laughter in her tone.

Rosemary threw her arms about both women and pulled them into a tight embrace.

"She'll do."

As Fontaine giggled, Annie squirmed out of the embrace and smoothed her palms over her skirt. "Perhaps it would be best, given my new position, if the two of you refrain from being so familiar with me."

Rosemary coughed before she could snort at the prim, nasal voice Annie had used.

"I'll show you *familiar*," Rosemary said. She nudged the door to the classroom firmly shut, glanced around to confirm no one was watching, then wrapped her arms around Fontaine. The sound of crunching paper made them both freeze.

"Oh!" Fontaine withdrew a flattened matchbox from her pocket and chuckled. "I suppose it was time to let go of it. It's not as if I'm a matchstick girl anymore."

"No," Rosemary said. "You're *my* matchstick girl."

Then she swept the headmistress into a deep kiss.

THE END

Author's Note

An estimated one in ten Canadians are descended from the more than 100,000 children brought to Canada from the United Kingdom between 1860 to 1948. As of this writing, the government of Canada has offered no apology for how many of these British Home Children were treated.

About the Author

Melissa lives in Regina, Saskatchewan; the capital city that feels like a small town. A passionate public speaker, board game enthusiast, and lover of all things Halloween, she spends her free time writing and spoiling her two cats.

Website –
melissakendall.ca

Amazon –
amazon.ca/stores/author/B0B8JVQKMC

Facebook –
facebook.com/MAKendallAuthor

Instagram –
instagram.com/makendallauthor

X (Twitter) –
twitter.com/MAKendallAuthor

TikTok –
tiktok.com/@makendallauthor